PRAISE FOR
I WILL NEVER SEE THE WORLD AGAIN

"Urgent...brilliant...a timeless testament to the art and power of writing amid Orwellian repression."
—*Washington Post*

"Remarkable...Altan's talent as a writer allowed him to communicate his experience in rich, haunting detail... Despite the oppressive, cruel darkness at the core of Altan's memoir, his words shine like bioluminescent creatures patrolling the abyss...brilliant."
—*NPR*

"The title of Mr. Altan's book is the statement of a brutal fact, rather than a cry of despair. There is not a smidgen of self-pity in the memoir's 212 pages. What emerges is this: You cannot jail my mind, and you cannot shut me up."
—*New York Times*

"[*I Will Never See the World Again*] speaks for itself with such clarity, certainty, and wisdom that only one thing needs to be said: read it. And then read it again...a radiant celebration of the inner resources of human beings... Its account of the creative process is sublime, among the most perfectly expressed analyses of that perpetually elusive phenomenon. And it is a triumph of the spirit."
—*The Guardian*

Lady Life

Lady Life

Ahmet Altan

Translated
from the Turkish by
Yasemin Çongar

OTHER PRESS
New York

First published in Turkish in 2021 as *Hayat Hanım*
by Everest Yayınları, Istanbul

Copyright © Ahmet Altan, 2021
English translation copyright © Other Press, 2023

Title-page art: Shutterstock / Essl

E. M. Cioran excerpt on page 123 from *The Trouble with Being Born*, trans. Richard
Howard. Copyright © 1976 by Seaver Books (NY: Arcade Books, 1998). Theodor
Adorno excerpt from "Is Art Lighthearted?" in *Notes to Literature*, vol. 2, ed. Rolf
Tiedemann, trans. Shierry Weber Nicholsen (NY: Columbia University Press, 1992).
Poetry extract on page 192 from "Musée des Beaux Arts" (1938) by W. H. Auden,
published in *Another Time* (New York: Random House, 1940).

Production editor: Yvonne E. Cárdenas
Text designer: Patrice Sheridan
This book was set in Arno Pro and DalyText by Alpha Design & Composition of
Pittsfield, NH

1 3 5 7 9 10 8 6 4 2

Library of Congress Cataloging-in-Publication Data
Names: Altan, Ahmet, author. | Çongar, Yasemin, 1966- translator.
Title: Lady life / Ahmet Altan ; translated from the Turkish by Yasemin Çongar.
Other titles: Hayat hanım. English
Description: New York : Other Press, [2023]
Identifiers: LCCN 2022042478 (print) | LCCN 2022042479 (ebook) |
ISBN 9781635422887 (paperback) | ISBN 9781635422894 (ebook)
Subjects: LCGFT: Bildungsromans. | Novels.
Classification: LCC PL248.A525 H3913 2023 (print) | LCC PL248.A525 (ebook) |
DDC 894/.3533—dc23/eng/20220907
LC record available at https://lccn.loc.gov/2022042478
LC ebook record available at https://lccn.loc.gov/2022042479

Lady Life

1

Lives were changing overnight. Everything was so rotten that people's roots in the past could no longer hold their present-day existence firmly in place. Like ducks in a shooting gallery, everyone lived with the possibility of being knocked over and disappearing with a single shot.

My own life changed overnight. Or rather, my father's life. As a result of events that didn't make much sense to me, a major country announced that it would be stopping the import of tomatoes, and just like that thousands of acres of land turned into a scarlet-colored dump. My father, with the foolhardiness one sometimes sees in people who resent their work, had invested all his money in a single crop, and so one sentence was enough to knock him over and drive him bankrupt. In the morning of a troubled night my father had a stroke.

We had fallen so hard that we couldn't even find the time to mourn him. As if suffering from a severe case of vertigo, we were able to see everything around us, including his death, but were unable to make any sense of it. A life we had thought would never change crumbled with a terrifying ease. We were free-falling in an unfamiliar void, and I didn't know what I was falling toward. That I would find out later.

We were left with the money in my mother's bank account and the one-acre flower greenhouse my father had bought for her amusement. "I will find a way to keep you at school, but gone are the days of luxury," she said. Studying literature on that vast, luminous campus had in fact become a luxury, but she wouldn't even hear of me dropping out.

My poor father had wanted me to become an agricultural engineer, but I insisted on majoring in literature. I suppose what determined my decision, as much as my fondness for the adventurous solitude within a fortress of novels, was my confidence that no choice could jeopardize my secure future life.

A week after my father's funeral I took the bus back to the city where my university was. The next morning I applied for student aid. I was a good student. They agreed to give me a scholarship.

Even so, I would no longer be able to pay the rent on the spacious three-bedroom house I shared with a friend. I found a room for rent on a street of dive bars where my schoolmates and I used to hang out. The room was in a six-story building from the nineteenth century, with purple wisteria covering its facade and small balconies with ornamental black wrought-iron railings. A wooden elevator still stood in its antique cage, but it didn't work. The place must have been built as a *han*;[1]

---

[1] A form of urban caravanserai in the Ottoman times, a *han* usually served as a hotel or a commercial compound for small businesses and wholesale shops. (*Translator's note*)

now it was used as a boardinghouse they rented out room by room.

Before I moved in, I put aside a few things to wear and, in a senseless act of fury, as if I was taking revenge for what had happened to us, sold all my clothes and books, my mobile phone, and computer to junk dealers at a very cheap price.

In the room there was a bed with a brass headboard, an old-style wooden nightstand, a tiny round table with a crack right in its middle that stood next to the balcony, a chair, and a mirror on the wall near the door. There was a toilet and a shower; together, they were the size of a small closet. There was no kitchen. A large room on the second floor was used as the communal kitchen. A long table made of rough-cut wood stood in the center, with two long benches on either side. A Frigidaire, at least fifty years old, grunted and growled, and shook at times. A white-tiled countertop, a sink with nineteenth-century bronze faucets with porcelain handles bearing the words CHAUD and FROID, a samovar that mysteriously always had tea on the boil, and a television set: these were the things we shared in our shared kitchen.

The room's small balcony was very nice. I would take out the chair, sit, and survey the cobblestone street. After seven at night, it started filling up. By nine you couldn't see the cobblestones anymore; a colorful crowd that breathed in and out as one surged and grew to cover the whole street. A cloud of anise, tobacco, and fried fish drifted up. There were sounds of laughter, whistles, joyful whoops. It was as if once you entered that scene, anything that happened outside was forgotten, and a transient bliss enveloped everyone. I watched from afar that fleeting vivacity in which I could no longer take part.

Tenants cooked their meals in the communal kitchen. They labeled their food before putting it in the fridge. No one touched anyone else's. In this building of penniless students, cross-dressers, Africans who produced and sold counterfeit luxury goods, young day laborers from the provinces, bouncers, and busboys who worked in nearby restaurants, there was a puzzling sense of order and peace. There was no manager to be seen, but everyone felt secure. Everyone guessed that some of the residents were involved in shady dealings outside the building, but that darkness never seeped in.

I didn't know how to cook. I didn't have enough money to buy proper meat or vegetables anyway, and I was too lazy to try to prepare food. I usually bought half a loaf of bread and cheese from the corner grocery and ate it at mealtimes. I suppose I resembled the rest of the "new poor" in the exaggerated and ridiculously inept way I tried to live through what had just happened.

I usually went down to the kitchen to have tea with my "meal." I had discovered that a bouncer with tattooed biceps who always went about in a black tank top cooked exotic dishes and served them to whoever was in the kitchen at the time. He made strange things like steak with pineapple and ginger-braised sea bass.

The building had an intelligence network as incomprehensible as its security system: everyone knew things about everyone else. I learned, without knowing how, that Gülsüm, the cross-dresser who lived next door to me, was in love with a married cook; the young man two doors down was called "Poet" by all the others; the portly black guy nicknamed "Mogambo" sold handbags during the day and worked as an escort at night; and one of the country boys had shot his cousin. It was as if the kitchen walls were whispering to keep us informed.

I greeted and exchanged a few words with everybody there, but befriended no one. The only person I enjoyed talking to was Tevhide. She was five, the only child in the building. With her short, roughly cut hair and deep-green eyes that looked at everything with curiosity, she shone like a drop of water.

The first time we met she gestured to me with her tiny finger to come closer and spoke into my ear as if she were sharing an astonishing secret. "Do you know," she asked, "that there is a number called one thousand five hundred?" "Really?" I acted surprised. "I swear. My friend told me today."

When I didn't see Tevhide and her father in the kitchen I would usually eat my bread and cheese, drink a few glasses of tea, and then go back upstairs to my room. I watched the street from the balcony for a while, then read a dictionary of mythology that I hadn't been able to bring myself to sell. An imagination spanning thousands of years that had given us gods worse than people, never-ending wars, romances, evils, envy and greed—it helped me forget the world in which I lived.

Fall, with its utter inevitability and glory, had been settling on the city. The weather was cooler, and classes had begun.

One evening, while I was eating in the kitchen, someone whose name I didn't know asked me if I wanted to work part-time after class. It didn't pay much, but the job was easy. I said yes without blinking. I needed every penny. He gave me a card that read FRIENDLY CASTING. The next day I went to the address on it.

That was a year ago. I didn't know then that life was so devoid of a hidden will, so subject to coincidence, that a single word, a mere suggestion, or a business card could change its course completely.

2

We went down four floors; the man pushed a door and let me in. I entered a luminous darkness.

As I stood at the entrance and looked straight ahead at a large round hall with a vaulted ceiling, an enormous shower of lights exploded in my vision. I closed my eyes. I opened them again slowly. The people and the things in the room looked like supernatural creatures under the bright, aggressive beams of light coming from the spots hanging on the ceiling. On the wall, purple, lavender, and blue flashes danced a turbulent ballet, as if trying to compete with the biting whiteness of the spotlights. Straight under the vault was a raised platform, about a foot from the floor. Rows of tables arranged in the shape of a half moon were on either side of the platform. Surrounding the tables were chairs covered in satin, with huge bows attached to their backs. To the left of the platform sat an orchestra of musicians in pink shirts.

There was a black visor on top of each spotlight—the bright-white rays were absorbed as they hit those visors, gradually dimming. The light grew darker as it permeated down from the vaulted ceiling and more or less extinguished by the time it reached the walls. The bright center stage was surrounded by darkness. Between the platform and the walls were several rows of tables. People sat there in groups of three or four. I took a seat at one of the empty tables in the back.

All at once music began to play. A man on the platform gave a signal, and the people at the tables began to clap. Through an invisible door next to the dancing lights a woman in a red evening dress came out and burst into song. She was fat. Her dress had a plunging neckline and was rather snug around her body, revealing her breasts, a round belly, and full hips. But she wasn't trying to conceal her heft—on the contrary, she wanted to draw attention to her curves.

All the singers that followed her were plump women in similarly tight evening dresses. The top of the turquoise dress of one was made with see-through lace, revealing her bra and her big, naked belly.

I had never seen so many fat and flirtatious women in one place. The aesthetic rules down here were different from those above. In the world up there, young women with small breasts, narrow hips, flat tummies, and long, thin legs were desirable, whereas here there was a taste for buxom women with wide hips, round bellies, broad and strong legs: these were mature women, curvaceous yet limber.

Images captured by cameras were shown on a large screen on the wall. The cameras didn't only show the singers: they also focused on the audience from time to time and sometimes even closed in on a single person among them. Those sitting at the tables on the platform were clearly veteran spectators. They seemed to be familiar with the rules of the place. Once, the camera zoomed in on one of the women sitting at those tables. Her face came up on the screen. Her wavy ginger-gold hair, her eyes etched with crow's-feet on the sides, her lips turned up at the corners were all remarkable. Yet her most striking feature was her expression. Her face had a teasing joviality about it, as if she were getting ready to crack a joke. She seemed on the brink of laughter. The face disappeared from the screen before I could look at it more.

She had attracted my attention at once. She, too, wore an evening dress with a plunging neckline. It was the color of honey, and it tightly embraced her plump body. When she got up to dance with others in the audience she did it smoothly, taking pleasure in what she was doing. Her bare shoulders shone under the lights. I was never good at guessing women's ages. My mother used to say, "Asians all look the same to white people, and people of a certain age all look the same to the young." She was right. Everyone above thirty sort of looked the same to me. Nonetheless, I guessed the woman in the honey-colored dress was between forty-five and fifty-five years old.

While most people there danced with exaggerated gestures so that the camera would turn to them, there was no pretension in the way she moved. She had gorgeous hips. Even though she shook and quivered with the most lustful moves she somehow seemed strangely untouchable. She was very attractive, but something about her, something I didn't quite grasp, was warning me not to get too close. I had never thought before that older women could be attractive. I was surprised, shaken up.

The show lasted about two hours. Once I saw my own face on the screen. Singers I had never heard of sang songs I had never heard. Most of them had good voices. Some among them sounded even better than some celebrity singers. Yet because they either lacked stamina and ambition or made the wrong decision at some point or other along the way, they had apparently taken a turn from the road leading to the summit of their art and ended up on this TV channel that only people in the slums watched. Still, they had no qualms about this. On the contrary, they seemed satisfied with their underground fame, a glory confined to the fringes of the city.

When the filming ended the spotlights were turned off, the blue, lavender, purple beams disappeared, and dim ceiling lights in the vault came on. Tables and chairs suddenly appeared old, the filth on the floor became visible, people's faces hung with exhaustion. A damp old-carpet smell took over the place.

The hall emptied slowly. Some went back to the greenroom to change out of their costumes, some left in haste. After a while I got up and exited the hall. On one side of the dusky corridor stood a row of plastic chairs. I sat in one of them. I didn't know where to go; after all that light, my room would look rather gloomy.

Those who had taken off their costumes in the back passed me by, one by one. The place grew quieter. The gray of the walls, with their peeling paint, got darker. I heard footsteps. It was the woman in the honey-colored dress. She had changed into a stylish tan trench coat, tightened with a belt around her waist, and dark-brown suede pumps. She had put her hair up.

As she passed by she looked at me out of the corner of her eye. Without a word she kept walking. The sound of heels began to recede. I felt a strange sense of disappointment. This baffled me. I didn't know I had hopes that could be frustrated. "I keep certain things even from myself," I mused as I listened to the click of her heels. She was going upstairs. She stopped. She turned back. The clicks began to get closer.

"She must have forgotten something," I thought. My head was bowed, my eyes fixed on the dirty floor tiles. Then I saw the dark-brown suede shoes on them. Their points turned toward me.

"What are you waiting for, looking so glum?"

My heart was racing so fast that for a second I thought I wouldn't be able to talk.

"Nothing," I barely managed to say.

"There's a good restaurant nearby," she said, "I'm going to have dinner there. Come if you'd like, we can eat together. Two is always better than one."

The first thing that crossed my mind was that I didn't have the money to pay for the meal. I don't know if she read this on my face or had decided to make the offer beforehand, but she added, "My treat."

"Sure."

I got up. We climbed the stairs and left the building without talking. We began to walk down the street. I was listening to the clicks of her heels. For some reason their rhythmic sound stirred my blood.

We went into a restaurant with jars of pickle and compote in its window. The place was empty, presumably because it was quite late. A waiter came:

"Welcome, Hayat Hanım,"[2] he said. "Where would you like to sit?"

"Let's sit in the garden."

Then, she turned to me.

"You won't be cold, will you?"

"I won't," I said.

It was a small garden, with a tiny pool with a fountain in the middle. A pergola covered it. The ground was concrete. Sculptures that had nothing in common, each one quirkier than the next, were randomly placed: one of the seven dwarfs with his red hat, a small giraffe, a plaster Venus, colorful ceramic birds hanging from the pergola, a cat that looked like a lynx, a princess in blue I thought to be Cinderella, an angel holding a star wand...

We sat at a table covered with a dark-red tablecloth. The waiter followed us, holding a notepad.

"What will you drink," Hayat Hanım asked me. In my mind, I was toying with her name. The way the waiter addressed her made me imagine her as a character from a medieval romance; *Hayat Hanım*, I repeated to myself in all the

---

[2] Hanım, meaning "lady" or "madam," is used in Turkish after the first name of a woman to address her in a formal manner. (*Translator's note*)

languages I could: *Hayat Hanım, Lady Life, Madame la Vie, Signora la Vita, Señora la Vida.*

"What will *you* drink?"

"Shall we drink rakı?"

"Sure."

She turned to the waiter.

"Please bring us double shots of rakı and some of your delicious mezes, but not so much that we can't enjoy a good bonito afterward."

She turned to me again.

"You eat fish, don't you?"

"I do."

I was floating away like a little stick thrown into the water.

After the waiter left, she said, "Come on, tell me. What do you do? Are you a student?"

"Yes."

"What are you studying?"

"Literature."

"I never read novels."

"Why not?"

"I don't know, I get bored...I already know the things novelists write. What I know about people is enough for me. I'm not going to learn much more than that from a writer."

"What are you interested in?"

"Anthropology," she said.

It was such an unexpected answer that I looked at her with my mouth wide-open, dumbfounded. I must have given the exact reaction she was aiming for. She laughed with the happiest laugh I had ever heard. You could hear various sounds in her laugh: morning birds, pieces of crystal, clear water flowing over the rocks, small bells hanging from a Christmas tree, little girls running about holding hands.

"I love that word," she said. "There is nothing more amusing than men's faces when I say it. I sometimes think they invented the word 'anthropology' just for the effect."

She continued to laugh.

"You aren't offended by my teasing you, are you?"

"No, I'm not."

I was about to say *I enjoy it*, but I didn't.

"What's your name?"

"Fazıl."

"It's a nice name."

"Your name must be Hayat, I heard the waiter say it."

"It's actually Nurhayat, but since childhood everyone has called me Hayat."

The waiter brought the rakı and the mezes. Hayat Hanım arranged the plates on the table with great care.

I looked at her. There was a mature light in her face, a face that wouldn't be deemed classically beautiful, but it had something more attractive than beauty: a nonchalance, a jocularity, and a wry compassion that seemed to embrace each and every nuance of humanity.

"What are you looking at?"

I felt myself blush. "I was lost in my thoughts," I said, hiding my eyes from her. She added water to the rakı glasses.

"Come on, eat," she said, "the mezes are good here. But don't fill yourself up, save some room for the fish too."

The mezes were indeed very tasty. I hadn't had a drink for a long time, and the rakı was already beginning to make me slightly tipsy. As I looked at Hayat Hanım, images of her dancing in her honey-colored evening dress flashed before my eyes.

Probing little by little, she had already learned my whole story by the time our fish was served. I told her everything I could, I suppose. I don't know how that happened, since I never like talking about myself. She listened to every word I said. Then she reached and touched my cheek with affection, a gesture so very calm and natural. For a while we remained silent. Her quietness was as ingenuous and expressive as her joviality—there was something therapeutic in it that eased the pain in you like the touch of a healer, at least that is how it felt to me.

When the waiter brought the fish, she said, "I only watch documentaries." I thought this was another one of her jokes, but she was serious.

"Why documentaries?" I asked.

"They're both fascinating and a lot of fun," she said. "Imagine: billions of people are covered by just twelve signs of the horoscope; thousands of years of experience taught people that the characteristics of their species could fit into twelve signs. In the meantime, there exist three hundred thousand kinds of bugs, and they're all different from one another. The species of fish, same story. You wouldn't believe what birds are capable of. And space, so mysterious and so terrifying... They've discovered in a single spot, in one single tiny spot on the space map, ten thousand galaxies. Isn't all of that exciting?"

That wry and endearing smile remained on her face as she talked, a smile that would have you believe God had created the entire universe to entertain Hayat Hanım and that she was enjoying it exactly the way she was meant to.

She had heard of Shakespeare and knew the phrase *to be or not to be.*

"Is that all there is," she said, "to the secret of human existence—a choice between life and death?"

"That line suggests indecision to me."

"Indecision? In my experience people are quite decisive."

"What are they so decisive about?"

"They are decisive about making dumb decisions. When you watch history documentaries you realize the same stupidity repeats itself without end."

"What sort of dumb decisions?"

"Come on, eat your fish," she said, as if she hadn't heard my question. "You're letting it get cold. Should we drink some more rakı?"

"Sure," I said.

She asked the waiter for two more rakıs.

She was certainly the most entertaining dinner companion a person could ask for. A bright and captivating conversationalist, her charm heightened by a sardonic disdain for everything and everyone—including herself. All manner of topics flitted around our table like fireflies.

She knew almost nothing about literature. She had never heard of Faulkner, Proust, or Henry James, but she knew that the general who defeated Hannibal in Carthage was Scipio; that Julius Caesar wore a red cape in battle; that the crust of the earth floats on a constantly moving ocean of fire; that some wood frogs completely freeze in winter, fall and break their icy bodies like a piece of china, but come back to life and are healed in the summer; that leopards fight with baboons; that termites take out their trash every night and have teams of garbage collectors; that ants engage in agriculture in the underground cities they build; that some birds use tools; that dolphins smack the sand with their tails in shallow waters to scare the fish, and when the fish jump they catch the poor little things in the air; that lions have an average life span of ten years; that a kind of spider goes fishing; that tiger beetles rape their females; that the stars explode and disappear on their own; that space keeps expanding nonstop; and many more things of the kind.

Her mind was like one of those quirky, cluttered stores where the cheapest junk is displayed side by side with the most precious antiques. As far as I could see, what she took away from all that information was an entertaining disdain, a cheerful indifference toward life. The way she talked would make you believe that for her life was a simple toy bought from a flea market: she could play and have fun with it, she didn't need to be afraid of breaking or losing it. I had never met anyone like her.

As we approached the end of our meal, she told me about praying mantises.

"The female bites off the male's head while mating," she said.

Then, looking right into my eyes, she added:

"The male keeps fucking the female after his head has been severed."

I felt my insides shake. It was the first time I heard a woman use the word "fuck" so easily.

When our meal was over, I felt dizzy standing up, I held on to the table, hoping she didn't notice.

After we left the restaurant she asked where I lived.

"Nearby," I said.

"Good."

She waved down a taxi, kissed me on the cheek, said "See you around," and got in. The car drove away.

The sky, taken over by a thick fog, reflected city lights back onto the streets, illuminating the night with a smoky brightness. The stone buildings, which housed in their small rooms illicit sweatshops, cardboard mills, firms involved in brand piracy, makers of plastic goods, offices of human smugglers disguised as travel agencies, had the city's hazy whiteness on their dark walls. On the ground floors of some were recently opened art galleries and fake antique shops selling replicas of furniture from a bygone age, their windows like oases of light. A case in arrested development, the gentrification of these streets had stopped all too suddenly, leaving behind a scene of tottering conflict.

She had invited me to dinner, but she didn't want me after all. I was left alone in the middle of the street on a night when everything could have happened but nothing did. Failing to be wanted had fractured the hidden mirror of my self-image. The "I" of my imagination was in shatters. What remained was my wobbly body. I now realized that a hidden self-image was what held me together: it made me who I was. However, I couldn't quite comprehend the fragility of that invisible mirror, the most essential piece of me, a pedestal on which my mind with its entire gallery of thoughts and emotions stood.

When had I become so weak that I collapsed with the first gust of wind, like a mulberry tree rotting inside? Where had that strong sense of confidence to safeguard me against another person's disapproval gone? She had wounded me at our first encounter, yet she had done literally nothing to hurt me. I would later understand that no one knew how to do nothing better than she.

When I told her later what I had gone through that night, "Goodness gracious," she said, in a voice that sounded full of regret, "I never thought you could be that fragile." But then she laughed with such an innocent joy that I could hardly believe she felt any regret for what she had done.

The jolt of disapproval revived all my sorrows, as if the cord holding together the bale of my misery was cut off, setting free all the pain and grief. My father's death, the suddenness of poverty, loneliness, desperation spread inside me like poison oozing from a snakebite.

Only later would I realize that like so many others I, too, brought to the surface my own collection of miseries to use as a shield against the real source of pain. Much later. Time would teach me that to understand such things as they were unfolding one needed a certain kind of experience, a maturity that was shaped by coming into collision with "real life," something I lacked then.

As I was approaching the boardinghouse I came upon a terrifying group of large bearded men with baseball bats in their hands. I had heard of them. They didn't attack restaurants packed with customers, but they followed people after leaving those restaurants, cornered and beat them on empty streets. Recently, they also attacked an art gallery in broad daylight, beat everyone inside, saying *You can't drink liquor here*, and destroyed the artwork. They hated all kinds of entertainment. They hated everyone who wasn't like them.

I was scared. Fear compounded my grief. Everything and everyone seemed to humiliate me. I turned to backstreets and took the long way home. I didn't stop by the kitchen. I went directly upstairs.

3

As I did every Saturday, I called my mother from the phone booth two streets down. She spoke with an effort to hide the grief that had settled in her voice since my father's death, but she couldn't withhold her worries about me.

"How are you, how is your health, are you eating, are you comfortable in the room you're renting, how is the school going, are you doing well in your classes, how are you doing with money?"

I said I was fine.

I could hear in her voice that my father's death—a fact that I still had trouble grasping—had already become firmly attached to her being. The night I rode the intercity bus back to school after the funeral, inhaling the smells of lemon cologne and plastic seat covers, I had realized suddenly that my father was indeed dead. "He died," I had thought.

My mother had hired an assistant, signed a deal with a couple of florists, and was now selling them fresh-cut flowers.

"I am making a little money," she said. "Do you need any?"

"No, Mom, I've got a job, I'm doing OK."

"You're not neglecting your studies, are you?"

"No, Mom."

I don't know why exactly, but after having talked to my mother I felt overwhelmed. I knew she was grieving and stressed, but there was nothing I could do about it.

She and my father were the happiest couple I had ever known. It was as if they shared an amusing secret nobody else knew. They always treated me with much love and affection; it would be an ungrateful lie to deny this. I always remember them side by side on the pier in front of the *yalı*,[3] laughing together as the sun set. I would go toward them, and they would see me and there would be a brief silence before they began talking to me. I always had the same odd feeling that they had left the room they had just been in and locked the door behind them—that they had come out of that room to be near me rather than letting me in. I could not go inside, they had to come out. Perhaps that wasn't the case, but that was the impression I had. I felt left out, yet didn't mind it so much. I, too, had established my own world—a world of books that left everyone else, including my parents, outside. There was a balance to our lives that allowed each one of us to feel good and happy. We were a beautiful family. At peace. One cannot learn much about life in happy, peaceful families, I understand this now: it is unhappiness that teaches us what life is about.

It was drizzling outside. I started to walk. I didn't know what to do. I had stopped seeing my old friends and I had no

---

[3] A house or mansion on the water, usually with its own pier. (*Translator's note*)

new ones. Holidays were hard for the lonely. I had come to learn that.

I would daydream about running into Hayat Hanım on the street. What if she appeared from around the corner... I knew this was more than unlikely, but hoping against hope I couldn't stop looking around. I was searching the streets for a woman. Would I do this when we were rich? Would I stroll alone on the streets lost in the dream of running into a woman whom I had met only once? Poverty had reduced me to this in such a short time, it had deprived me of so much more than just cash. Like a baby turtle whose shell had been removed from his body, I was helpless, unsheltered, weak. The faintest breeze, the slightest drop in temperature, the tiniest leaves of grass, the edges of the smallest rocks, all had a major effect on my body and mind as though they represented a major change in my physical circumstances. I quivered a little more with each such shift. I could never conceive the possibility that *just like that* my thick and warm shell could be removed. It embarrassed me to see how little was left behind from what I used to be, once they took away the money.

I decided to go to the old booksellers' arcade. It was always packed with people. I could just blend in. The arcade smelled like stone, dust, and old paper—it was dim inside and, contrary to my expectations, empty. Only a few people wandered from one store to another. Several shops were closed, their windows plastered over with old newspapers. The arcade resembled a patient on his deathbed. I asked a shopkeeper what had happened to the place. "No one comes here anymore," he said, and shrugged. "They will soon demolish the building anyway." People had abandoned books. I never thought this could happen. No matter what, there were people who would always love books, but they weren't there today.

I entered a store. Inside an old shopkeeper was reading. He raised his head from his book and looked at me, then without a word returned to the page. As I was browsing, a picture hanging amid the floor-to ceiling towers of old books caught my eye. It had a thin frame, its glass dull with age. It was a reprint of August Sander's photograph *Three Farmers on Their Way to a Dance*. The expression on the faces of the farmers, who were dressed in dark suits to go out to have fun, was astounding, the extreme severity of their facial lines betraying the tension they felt in getting ready for a night of great entertainment.

I pointed at the print and asked how much it was. I guess one could hear in my voice the nervous generosity of a man ready to spend all of his riches on a picture. It wouldn't take much to guess that what I had in my pocket was hardly a fortune.

The man raised his head and gave me a pensive look. He stared at me without a word. I almost saw in his eyes time flowing backward without haste, years piling back on each other toward the past, him arriving at a place where he had found perhaps great love or solid friendship.

"It is yours," he said.

I was staggered. I asked again without even noticing I was being rude.

"How much?"

He repeated in the same calm voice: "It is yours."

He got up, took the frame down, wrapped it in thick, brown paper, and handed it to me. I was surprised, embarrassed, and happy. It wasn't the print that gave me so much joy, but the man's subtle, completely unemphasized generosity. A friendliness his face didn't reveal.

I left the shop in a good mood. My emotions changed abruptly; they were all over the place. I bought half a loaf of bread with some cheese and went back to the han. I removed the wrapping paper and put the frame on my bedside table, leaning it against the wall. The room had changed at once. A single photograph altered the room. The place had now become my home.

I took my meal and went down to the kitchen. There were many people at the dining table. They were watching a soccer game. It had been a long time since I had watched a game, even though I loved soccer. Oddly, I had forgotten how much I liked it. I poured myself tea, sat down at the table, and began to watch. Among those looking at the screen was Gülsüm in her slit skirt and heavy makeup, clearly prepared to go to work. She followed the game with great enthusiasm. "Bullshit," she said once, "that's a foul, plain as day." I looked at her in awe, but no one else did; they seemed to be used to her commentary. After a short while Gülsüm spoke again: "If he doesn't take out the right-back he'll lose the game." The team's manager changed the right-back soon after. Someone at the table turned to Gülsüm and said, "They should make you the manager," to which she responded: "I've got the knack to get people off their asses; they'll play like no one has ever played." Everyone laughed. I looked down and took a bite of my bread.

I went up to my room before the game was over. There was a recording session at the TV studio that evening. Excited about the prospect of seeing Hayat Hanım, I was mentally going over what I'd say and do if we went to dinner again, rehearsing various phrases. This time I wasn't going to act like a silly schoolboy.

When I went out the street had begun to get crowded. I walked to the studio, went down four floors, and entered that luminous darkness.

Hayat Hanım wasn't there. She didn't come that night. I had been persuaded that she would come there every night, although no one had told me that. I felt wronged. Betrayed. Humiliated. I was smart enough to know these feelings were preposterous, but I wasn't strong enough not to feel them. My emotions were like a herd of mustangs running amok. I couldn't stop them; they galloped in various directions.

Plump women in tight dresses sang and danced with lustful and unapologetically inviting moves. To dance better, some took off their shoes and left them in the middle of the stage. A woman taking off her shoes to dance barefoot evoked intimacy. I realized that as I was watching them.

A stubby clarinet player with dark glasses and a white fedora, his hair tied in a ponytail, approached to play closer to the singers every now and then. He was rather short, almost the same height as his clarinet. His pink shirt hung loose over his trousers.

During the intermission I went out to the corridor with everyone else. From a small snack counter at the end of the corridor I bought a tea and a grilled cheese sandwich. I sat in a plastic chair near the wall. Two women sat in the chairs next to mine; they wore pencil skirts and makeup too heavy for their age. Their tight, sleeveless blouses looked like they were glued to their skin. They ignored me and kept talking to each other as if I weren't there.

"Who decides who sits on that platform?" one of them asked. "The cameras show the audience on the platform more than anyone else."

The other woman laughed. "To sit there you have to cajole the assistant director, he decides who sits where."

"Show me that assistant director, let me talk to him." She seemed quite self-confident.

I was embarrassed by what I had heard. Also angry. I took those words for an insult to Hayat Hanım. Those two women were like neither the ladies I knew nor the female characters in the books I read. There was something in their banality that I found attractive, and the moment I realized this I got up at once and went inside the main hall.

When the session was over, I left before anyone else. I walked home alone. I was afraid of running across those men with bats, but they didn't seem to be around, perhaps because it was still too early for them to come out. I made my way through the crowd on the street that led to the han, bumping against people and rushing as if I was worried about chancing upon an old friend.

The people on the street were mostly young. The girls smelled nice, their sweet perfumes reaching me through the street's heavy air.

I went up to my room. The three farmers were there. I had forgotten about them. Clad in black suits, they were on their way to a dance. I went out on the balcony and watched the people outside. Even though it was the weekend the crowd looked smaller than usual.

Hayat Hanım didn't come the next day either. The session began. The lamps in the hall were turned off, the spotlights came on, the blue-lavender-purple rays shone on the stage. As the first singer was singing I heard the door behind me open and someone enter and sit somewhat shyly at the other side of my table. It was a girl. I couldn't see her face well, since she kept looking straight at the stage. She perched on the edge of her chair. She didn't move. She didn't applaud.

When it was time for the intermission and the lamps in the hall were back on, I turned to look at her. At that moment, she had also turned toward me. A noble face. This would be the first thing anyone would think at the sight of her: She has a noble face. A nose with sharp edges, somewhat fleshy on the sides, carved out of smooth marble by a master sculptor. Thickish eyebrows that got thinner toward the ends. Slightly bulging eyes framed with lots of lashes. Large black pupils that looked straight through you, lost in private thoughts that are none of your business. A wide and smooth forehead.

Luxuriant black hair falling on her shoulders in shiny tresses. Lips with an extremely serious expression, although also intimating sensuality. And a look from above, a singular, humbling stare that was settled in all her facial features.

The contrast between the girl's face and the images around us was so incredible and unanticipated that for a second I thought I had passed through a crack in my mind and fallen into the fantastic world of the subconscious, with no room for reality. This face could not possibly exist here. But it was here. It had been dropped here from somewhere else.

"They sell grilled sandwiches and tea at the snack counter outside," I said. "I'll buy one for myself, would you like one too?"

"Are the sandwiches any good?"

"They're OK."

"Do we have to eat in the corridor? Can't we eat here?"

She clearly didn't want to go and mingle with the studio audience. I didn't know the rules of the place, but I said, "We can eat here."

"All right," she said.

I went out to the corridor. There was a disconcerting buzz. The crowd looked weird. Some women had fancy gowns on, some wore cheap cotton dresses. Most of the men were old; well-combed and sporting ties that didn't match their suits, they eyed the women flirtatiously. I saw the two women from the day before cornering the show's assistant director. The guy had a cheeky smile. The women had wriggled themselves into him. One of them kept feeling the guy's shirt collar between her two fingers as she talked.

I turned away.

I bought two teas and two grilled cheese sandwiches at the snack counter, put them on a plastic tray, and took it inside. The girl was sitting exactly as I had left her; she seemed not to have made a single move or taken a single breath. She said *merci* as I gave her the sandwich and tea. I had no doubt she would say *merci* in the same exact tone to her housemaid.

"Are you a student?" I asked.

"Yes."

"What are you studying?"

"Literature," she said reluctantly, as if not wanting to talk about it.

"I am studying literature too," I said eagerly.

She gave me an uncertain look, doubting and curious in equal measure. She bit at her sandwich daintily and looked down, buried in her thoughts.

"If you could have written any fifteen pages of literature from the whole of history, which fifteen pages would you choose?"

I knew this was a test similar to that picture of a hat in *The Little Prince*. We would become friends if I gave the right answer; if not, she would lose all interest in me. My first instinct was to find the kind of answer she might like. But that was impossible to know, so I gave up and went on to tell her what I really thought.

"The 'Time Passes' chapters in *To the Lighthouse*."

I saw the immediate look of amazement on her face turn into a smile.

"Good choice!"

At that moment, the audience came back into the hall. The lamps went out, and the spotlights came back on.

"What's your name?" I quietly asked.

"Sıla," she said. "What is yours?"

"Fazıl."

"Cool."

We turned to face the stage. I saw those two women seated at one of the tables on the platform. The session ended, and without a word, Sıla and I left together.

Outside, I asked her: "Where are you heading to?"

"I'll take the bus from here, but we can walk a little before I do. I can get on the bus farther down the road."

While we walked she told me her story. My reference of *To the Lighthouse* had earned me her unconditional trust. She had decided I wasn't one of *those people*, the kind she referred to with disgust.

"The police raided our house one night," she said.

Her father used to be the chief proprietor of a major company; they used to live in a villa in the middle of an orchard.

"The trees were so beautiful," she said.

A minor partner who owned merely 2 or 3 percent of her father's company was arrested on charges of "conspiracy against the government," and the authorities had taken over her father's entire business.

"Is that even possible?" I asked.

"Nowadays it is."

We walked quietly for a while.

"It took them four hours to search our house," she said. "Then they told us to leave the place immediately. They only allowed us to take a single suitcase. They threw us out in the middle of the night. As we were leaving they searched the suitcase as well as my mother's purse and mine. They took away our credit cards, but that didn't matter much since they had already confiscated all our savings in the bank."

She spoke in a calm, flat voice. Every now and then she would take a long pause before she began talking again. Her unhurried and easy manner of speech, which reminded me of a slow-flowing river, somehow managed to keep one's attention alive. The lack of excitement in her manner was exciting to listen to. Profoundly beautiful, like the tides on the seabed, sealed off from the world outside, her voice seemed to emerge from the depths only to share a secret, creating in the listener a spellbinding effect intensified by the ineffable yet unmistakable whiff of intelligence that penetrated her words.

She spoke with the indifference of solitude, one brought about by the keen belief that there is no other person on earth with whom one's emotions could resonate.

"At midnight we left the house with that single suitcase. My father tried to object, but the cops said, 'Let it go now or we'll arrest you right away.' They didn't let him call his lawyers. They even took both of my parents' cell phones, I don't know why, but they didn't take mine... There was a park close to our house. We went there."

She was quiet for a good while.

"I suppose I'll never forget that night in the park," she said. "We sat under a tree, holding on to our suitcase … That morning we were wealthy, even at dinnertime that day we were wealthy, but by midnight we had become homeless, penniless paupers."

She chuckled.

"Like Cinderella, our lives turned into a pumpkin at midnight."

Then she got serious again.

"We didn't know where to go. My mother suggested we go spend the night at some friends' house, but my father said they would be afraid to let us in their home. 'We should not put people in a position where they would have to turn us down,' he said. We knew he was right. In fact, no one offered to help us. You know what? Rich people are cowards, the more money they accumulate the more fears they have. But you only realize this once you become poor. When you're wealthy that inner fear feels natural."

She paused and said "cowards" as if whispering to herself, and then she continued:

"My father has a cousin, Hakan. He used to be a research assistant at the university, and my father had bought him a studio flat. Hakan went to Canada for a year on a scholarship and gave me his key before he left. He said I could have the place cleaned regularly and stay there whenever I wanted to study with friends."

Whenever I wanted to study with friends—I considered what kind of study would require a special studio apartment but didn't say anything.

"I told my parents I had Hakan's keys and that we could go to his place. My dad asked me how come I had Hakan's keys. Fathers will always be fathers, I guess. My mom said, 'Muammer, is this a problem now?' It started to rain. We went to Hakan's place. Even the bathrooms in our house were bigger than Hakan's entire flat. Just two rooms, and no doors between them. We settled in. We still live there ... The next day, my dad contacted a corporate lawyer and asked him to object to the confiscation of our assets. The man called him back that night with the news that the judge had rejected the appeal without even reading the file. 'Let it go,' he said to my father, 'thank God that you weren't arrested.' I guess my father still has some money abroad, but they took away our passports too. We can't leave the country ... Dad looked for a job for a long time. He got hired as an accountant in a couple of small companies, but each time he was soon asked to leave for no apparent reason."

"What is he doing now?"

"He prepares the waybills for middlemen in a wholesale vegetable market. They don't pay him much for this. He also gets some bruised fruits and vegetables."

She gave a sarcastic laugh that seemed to imply a desire to avenge everything they had been subjected to.

"My mother is now an expert in sorting out the edible parts of bruised fruits."

"How did you manage to stay in school?" I asked.

Earlier she had told me she went to a highly reputable and very expensive college, a rival of my school.

"My dad had paid a year's tuition in full. So there's no problem for now…If I stay here next year I'll apply for a scholarship."

"Are you thinking of going away?"

"I'm trying to get my passport back. If I can, I'll go to Canada, where Hakan is."

"What about your parents?"

"They want me to go too. After a while, they'll also come if they can. But without me they'll be a bit better off here. Living all together in such a cramped place is equally hard for them."

"How did you find out about this job?" I asked.

Someone at her college whose name she couldn't remember had told her about the job and sent her to the Friendly Casting company.

"I may have seen the wife of one of my father's former colleagues in the audience," she said, "but I am not sure."

Then she asked me:

"How did *you* end up here?"

I told her my story.

"So we meet in exile, huh?"

"Yes," I said. "We met in exile."

That's what I said, but in fact I imagined us as two baby turtles with their shells removed. Like two naked turtles we wriggled against one another, trying to nestle. If we still had had our shells they would have hit against each other and kept us apart. We wouldn't have told our stories so soon. We were both taught not to tell. They used to write our identities on the flesh of our backs and then slip the hard shells on tightly. In those days, we wouldn't have given ourselves away so readily.

We walked a bit more, then she said, "I am exhausted, let me take the bus from here." We began to wait at the bus stop. She was quiet. Pensive. Then, suddenly she knew what to say: "Let me give you my number, save it on your phone, we'll talk."

"I don't have a cell phone."

For a moment she gave me a doubting look; I guess she thought I didn't want to tell her my number. "I sold my cell phone," I said anxiously, and added with hurry: "Give me your number, I'll call you from a landline."

"Will you be able to remember it?"

"I will."

She gave me her phone number. I knew I owed this to the *Lighthouse*.

"When can I call you," I asked.

"Whenever you like."

Her bus came. She got on it. It drove away.

It was Sunday, so the streets around the TV studio were deserted. I walked back to the han. I entered the kitchen. The bodyguard with the black tank top was cooking.

"Would you like to eat," he asked.

"What are you making?"

"Hash and eggs," he said, "I'm hungry."

"Really? With *nothing funky* in the mix?"

"Nope... I said I was hungry, didn't I?"

"Why don't you have yourself one of those pineapple dishes you make all the time?"

"No," he said with a chuckle.

"I'd love some hash and eggs," I said.

He brought the shallow pan in which he cooked the food to the table. He also took out a loaf of bread, broke it into two with his large hands, and gave me half. We began to eat, dipping our bread into the pan.

"Why don't you make dishes like this more often?" I asked. "It *is* delicious. The best hash and eggs ever."

"I want to open a small place," he said. "For the upper crust, though...A restaurant that serves the rich guys the kind of dishes no other place does."

We ate up, polishing the bottom of the pan with the last bits of our bread. He enjoyed watching me eat with such appetite.

"Let me put on some coffee," he said. "It goes well after a meal like this."

While we were drinking our coffee Tevhide and her father came in and I saw Bodyguard light up as much as I did at the sight of them. He rose immediately and asked Tevhide if she was hungry: "Can I make you hash and eggs?"

Tevhide talked to everyone she saw in the building, asked them questions, befriended them. Everyone who had the chance to cook a decent meal for himself in the kitchen offered to share it with Tevhide and her father Emir, who always took what was offered and put it on Tevhide's plate but never ate any of it himself. Whenever he took some food that was offered and gave it to his daughter I always saw a tiny lilac-colored vein twitch under his left eye. He was in his thirties, with a lucid, almost transparent face and a polite manner of speech that gave away a background of solid education. He treated his daughter as if she were an adult and answered all her questions with utmost seriousness.

He obviously didn't belong here, in this place. Someone had pulled away the backdrop that used to inform him about who he was, transporting him to an entirely different scene. Like most of us he had lost his past and was now wandering like a ghost in a mystifying haze.

"Hash and eggs? What's that?" asked Tevhide.

Whenever she heard a new phrase she would immediately ask what it meant and then make a point of using it in conversation over the next couple of days. Her vocabulary was remarkably rich for her age. Emir told her what hash and eggs were.

"I don't want any," she said. "I'll drink milk."

We all smiled. Her directness about what she did and didn't want made us smile every time.

"You didn't say *thank you*," said Emir.

Tevhide turned to Bodyguard and said *thank you*. Emir took the bottle marked "Tevhide" from the fridge and poured milk for his daughter. We sat quietly for a while. As the silence stretched I asked Bodyguard: "How is work?"

"The neighborhood isn't as upbeat as it used to be," he said. "Those scoundrels run around with their bats and scare away the customers."

"Won't the cops do anything?"

He looked up, and once he was sure no one else was around he leaned toward me: "No one wants to mess with those men."

Emir, uncomfortable with such matters being discussed in the presence of his daughter, said, "We should go." After they had left, I went upstairs to my room.

The farmers were going to a dance. Soon I fell asleep.

I dreamed about Hayat Hanım in her honey-colored dress. She was looking at me while she danced.

4

"*Sentimental Education* and *Daisy Miller* are two novels written in the same era. Flaubert's *Sentimental Education* was published in 1869, Henry James's *Daisy Miller* came out nine years later, in 1878. And actually, neither of these novels is as brilliant as their fame suggests."

There was a roar in the lecture hall. Thanks to her provocative attitude, Nermin Hanım's classes were the best-attended ones at the university—she was always ready to say things about literature no one else would dare to. In her black skintight jeans, red stilettos, and crisp white shirt with its collar turned up, she walked on the campus as a clear and present challenge to "academia." Her face was narrow, with eyes that were too big for it, her stiff black hair raised on her head like a bush. Her reading glasses were always in her hand, and when she talked she kept clicking their temples. "Literature can't be taught," she said during her first lecture, "I cannot teach you literature. What I *will* teach you is what one badly needs in dealing with literature, and that is literary courage. Don't try to exist by repeating other people's phrases. Be brave. Literature takes courage; great writers emerge from among those who write with courage. This is what you'll learn in this class: literary courage."

She did keep her word. In each lecture she shook up the entire class, all our beliefs and paradigms.

"Now," she said, "we'll look at the concept of freedom in those two books. Both of them feature free women ... We find women who are free to live their lives according to their own wishes in *Sentimental Education,* and *Daisy Miller* is based on the typology of a free woman. What we should note here is that the idea of freedom, of living freely, manifests itself quite differently in these books. In *Sentimental Education,* women live a life that's very much regulated by do's and don't's, and while they don't challenge the validity of those rules, they quietly violate and circumvent them, developing their own secretive, unapproved ways of existence. Daisy Miller, on the other hand, rebels outright against the system of prohibitions. She designs a life of freedom for herself ... We see here the difference between living freely through submission and living freely through defiance ..."

I loved this universe where the greatest act of bravery was to criticize a book by Flaubert, a universe where one made sense of concepts, ideas, and emotions merely through the characters in a novel. I wanted to live in that universe. I belonged to that universe. My biggest dream was to spend my life among people who loved literature, who taught it, who discussed it. Each lecture by Nermin Hanım made me a little more aware of this desire of mine. Literature, with its genuineness and capacity for amusement, surpassed life. Literature was not safer than life, however, perhaps it was even more dangerous. Authors' biographies had taught me that writing could bring serious harm. Yet when it came to honesty, literature had no rival. Kaan Bey,[4] the professor of the history of literature, once said, "Literature looks into the infinity of the human soul." I could hear his hoarse voice in my head: "It's a telescope through which you can see each and every bright star and each and every black hole of the human spirit."

From books, I had learned to surveil people quietly, myself included. I knew already that the human soul was not an undivided whole. It consisted of various pieces that were held together somehow. And at the seams, there was always, in everyone, some leakage. Whenever I began to ruminate like this, I could see myself always hurrying to get away from my classmates to avoid having to tell them I had now become a poor man, to keep this truth from them as long as I could, all the while knowing full well that this was a stupid thing to do. I was afraid they would feel sorry for me, that they would look down on me. At the same time, I realized that my fear made me even more pitiful. Owning up to the truth would make me stronger, I knew that, and more respectable even, yet knowing that wasn't enough to dissuade me from getting away from my classmates as fast as I could. This was one of my leaky seams, one that wasn't easy to mend. Both my poverty and my efforts to hide it embarrassed me.

---

[4] Bey, used after a first name, is a formal form of addressing a man in Turkish. (*Translator's note*)

What Nermin Hanım had said in class occupied my thoughts. I realized that I had never before seriously considered what freedom was. An inquisition was unleashed in my mind: *Am I free?* The question had not gradually emerged in my mental monologue, no, it had appeared out of nowhere and plastered itself on the enormous billboard of my imagination: *Am I free?* Scarier than the question was the answer to it: *No, I am not.* To be followed by an even more unsettling query: *Will I ever be free?*

By each step of this mental inquisition, I was reduced to a tiny piece of the puzzle that was my life. I couldn't fit into the picture, I couldn't make it whole. I merely reacted to incidents, I did not act by my own will. I had no agency, no ability to provide an orientation to my life, neither through submission nor defiance. I was nothing. My presence on earth didn't change anything.

How could I not realize this until now? How come it had never occurred to me to ask these questions before? Had I heard Nermin Hanım's ideas about freedom a year ago, would I have been as rattled as I was now, or would my family's wealth have prevented me from seeing the truth? Did other people ask themselves such questions? Or had one to fall off a cliff and be shattered to pieces in order to examine oneself the way I now did? Did people grasp the meaning of freedom only when they were broken? What should I be doing now? What must I do? How could I go on living with the self-knowledge that I was incapable of making life move even an inch?

Something slowly changed inside me; ideas and emotions I hadn't fully grasped before collapsed and were replaced by new ones. I discovered new questions, and their potential answers horrified me.

That evening I went to the TV studio. Hayat Hanım was there. From where I sat I could see her ginger-gold hair and the compassionate disdain of her smile. She was in her honey-colored dress, engulfed in a blaze of burning gold under the spotlights. Soon after the lamps were turned off Sıla also arrived. She turned around before sitting down and gave me a smile.

A woman in a jazzy dress of red and green was singing. A four-fingers-thick sash embroidered with sequins stretched down from her shoulders to her groin in the shape of the letter V. It was like an illuminated sign pointing at a target.

The camera stayed on Sıla and me for a moment; our faces appeared on the gigantic screen. I felt a strange sense of guilt. I hadn't committed a crime or done anything wrong, really, but I felt culpable all the same.

They ended the session without breaking for an intermission. The audience began to leave. I had not moved. Sıla got up and waited for me to get up too. So I did. Side by side we went out to the corridor. People seemed to be flowing down the stairs on either side of us. They were critiquing the session among themselves: whom the camera shot most, who danced how, whose dress was terrible, who tried to attract the camera's attention with exaggerated gestures.

Sıla gave me an impatient look. At that moment I heard a voice call my name. I turned around. Hayat Hanım was rushing toward us through the crowd. Sıla looked at her, then turned to look at me. Hayat Hanım had already caught up with us. "OK, then, this is my cue," said Sıla. I didn't say a word. For the shortest of moments all three of us stood there without the slightest move. I could smell the dampness of the carpets. All of the sounds around us were humming in my ears. Hayat Hanım was looking at me, I was looking down, and then Sıla turned around and left. I looked at her from behind, feeling something that resembled both pain and shame, but couldn't make myself move.

"How are you?" asked Hayat Hanım.

"Good, thank you, how are you?"

"If you're free, wait for me and we can grab some dinner."

"I'll wait," I said.

"I'll change and come back right away."

I sat in a plastic chair and waited. Hayat Hanım had not asked about Sıla. But I was sure she had seen us together on the large screen. She would always deny this, although she never lied to me otherwise. Whenever I probed about an incident whose details could upset me, she would give me a slightly distanced look—a warning sign that she was about to tell me the truth. At times I retrieved my questions, and sometimes, braving pain, I demanded an answer. She lied to me only that day, about that minor, unimportant detail. In fact, that day when Sıla and I appeared on the screen I had immediately glanced at Hayat Hanım and found her eyes fixed on our image. In later days, whenever I raised the issue with an obscure desire of cornering her, she always repeated the same line: "Why would I ever be looking at the screen? You're making this up." Whenever she said this, an unfamiliar smile would appear on her face, unrehearsed and discomposed, as if a confession was about to tear it apart momentarily. Her unusually still grin seemed to confirm what she denied with words.

That evening we went to the restaurant with sculptures again. This time she had not put her hair up.

"You didn't show up during the weekend."

"I had things to do," she said simply, and left it there. I was annoyed with Hayat Hanım but couldn't explain why. There wasn't an obvious reason for it. As if going through the things in an old chest, I dug deeper and deeper to look for the cause of my irritation. "You seem preoccupied," she said. "No," I shrugged with a laugh, and went on to tell her about the old bookseller who gave me the picture.

"There are such people," she said. "But not very many."

She smiled with that unconcerned smile of hers: "The fools who fully grasp the value of their possessions are far greater in number.

"Did you know," she continued, "that once every twenty thousand years, the earth tilts ever so slightly on its axis of rotation around the sun?"

I had never heard of such a thing.

"I didn't know that," I said.

"When the earth tilts, the Great Sahara turns into a forest... It remains a forest for twenty thousand years... Then the earth tilts again and the forest turns back into a desert."

I looked at her face, wondering if she was pulling my leg.

"Honestly," she said. "I watched a documentary on this. They found remnants of ancient forests in the Sahara."

She took a sip of her rakı.

"To me it doesn't seem wise to take anything too seriously while we all live on a wobbly piece of rock."

"How can we live without taking things seriously?"

"How can you live *by* taking things seriously?"

She touched the back of my hand with her finger.

"One should always keep certain things in mind. First of all, we live on a wobbly, unstable piece of rock. Second, we are creatures with very short life spans. Third..."

She stopped.

"Third?"

"You find out the third thing yourself," she said. "Come on, eat a little, the mezes are great."

She didn't like to argue about things, she didn't try to persuade me one way or another, she said what she wanted to say and didn't care about what I made of it.

She was wearing a plum-colored, snug-fitting dress. When she leaned against the table I could see the shadowy depths of her cleavage.

I suspected Sıla might have been upset. The thought flickered like a specter on a shaded street; I knew it would keep reappearing.

As we were leaving the restaurant, I knocked into the Cinderella sculpture. I was nervous.

"Let's walk a little," she suggested. "The weather is nice."

We began to walk. I listened to the sound of her heels. We didn't talk. She seemed pensive. After we had walked quite a bit, she stopped abruptly and said, "I'm tired, let's get into a cab." I hailed one. We got in. She gave her address to the driver. She sat on one end of the back seat, I on the other, a gap between us. The cab stopped in front of a six-story building on a road leading downhill from the affluent part of town to a middle-class neighborhood. I paid the cab fare. She didn't object.

She unlocked the door of the apartment building. We entered. We got into an elevator with a shiny chrome door. We didn't touch, but we could feel each other. I could smell her lily-like scent. On the top floor we got off.

Her apartment was surprisingly plain. There was an armchair, upholstered in beige velvet, whose wear gave it away as her favorite spot, with a small side table beside it; a three-seat hunter green sofa set against the wall; a dining table toward the back of the room with fresh-cut flowers in a vase on it; and a huge television that seemed to be the most expensive piece of furniture in there. Two lamps, one next to the armchair and the other near the sofa, gave the place a serene light.

"Sit down," she said. "I'll make coffee."

I sat down on the sofa. A little later she came back with coffee. She sat in the armchair, crossed her legs. Her skirt went up a bit. I quietly swallowed. I didn't know what to do or what to say exactly. She was seducing me, yet I even failed at being seduced properly.

"Your apartment is very nice," I said.

My voice came out husky.

"You like it?"

"Yes, it's very nice."

The flat smelled like flowers. The curtains were drawn. She was smiling at me. She looked amused. We drank our coffee in silence. I felt like I had to say something but couldn't find anything to say. I didn't know if she expected me to make the first move. I was frozen, incapable of anything but sitting still.

When she drank up her coffee she left the cup on the side table. She stood up and said *come on* with a calm voice, then walked toward the back of the apartment. I followed her. I looked at the back of her knees as we walked. We passed a longish corridor and went to her bedroom. A small night lamp near the large bed had been turned on.

Slowly she took off her clothes. She took her time getting out of each garment, as if undressing itself was an act of pleasure for her. By the time she had gotten naked I still had my shirt on. I was lost watching her. Her body was younger than her face. She got into bed, looked at me, and said *come on* again in a teasing tone—"Are you going to stand there like that?" I undressed quickly.

She made love in the same manner she undressed: softly, without haste. She steered me with gentle touches. Her gentle touches taught me what to do. I obeyed them. Like a master archer she released the arrow only when the bow was fully drawn, and all at once we picked up the pace, moaning and screaming. I was lost in a delicate fragrance of lilies, taken over by an unsettling feeling, as if I were free-falling and fly-ing all at once.

The following eleven days were an entirely new life, a sep-arate universe that nestled between two parentheses within the life I used to know: a universe with its own private gravity, its own private time, light, and smell. It had rules I had not known, habits I had not learned, pleasures I had not experi-enced before.

Hayat Hanım took me into her life with docility and ease, the same way she gave me her body. I settled there without the slightest hindrance. There was something troubling in her lack of restraint, though: that innate casualness of hers must have fueled the anxieties and jealousy of mine that would later emerge. I didn't know then that entering a life was akin to setting foot in an underground maze of magic spells. Once you entered someone else's life you couldn't leave as the same person you were before you entered. I thought I could live my life in the kind of safety reading a novel provided me—that no matter how much I was affected by what was happening, I'd be able to release myself of its emotional grip whenever I wanted.

To me she was a mythological goddess whose name was yet to be added to the dictionary. I couldn't stop touching her. I felt a chill in my body when I wasn't close to her: I wasn't able to stay away.

At home she walked around in what looked like a beach dress, with thin straps, that revealed most of her bosom and ended just below her hips. She wore slightly heeled slippers with black leather straps. When I approached her anywhere in the apartment swallowing nervously, she didn't say *no*. Instead, she teased me with a grin: "You were on me just now, don't you ever tire of it?" Along with that provocative tease, I could hear in her voice the satisfaction she had in seeing the evidence of her own sex appeal. I saw the lines under her eyes, around her mouth, the wrinkles on her neck and under her armpits; near the bulge of her breasts, I saw the stretch marks on her soft underbelly; I saw her thickening waist. The beauty of her youth may have been disintegrating, but these flaws made her even more attractive. I wouldn't have liked her to be younger and more beautiful—I knew that in my heart and soul. I remembered Proust's words: *Let us leave pretty women to men with no imagination.*

I was under the enigmatic spell of her body. I felt I had to touch her, hold her, embrace her to feel alive. Just seeing her from a distance was enough to arouse me. I'd become obsessed with her flesh in a single night, yet I wasn't in love. As it happens, I had experienced neither sexual obsession nor love before and didn't know how to distinguish one from the other. Nonetheless I believed I wasn't in love with her. *I can't be in love with someone who doesn't care for literature*, I kept saying to myself. I didn't know then what Iris Murdoch, when asked what love was, had to say: "It is the extremely difficult realization that something other than oneself is real."

Sometimes I had these passing reflections, not emotions, not thoughts, but something in between, half-formed, strange, hard to grasp and equally hard to explain: had I also not had to have heard what I would say to Hayat Hanım I could have expressed some of those feelings. I didn't flinch at the idea of her knowing how I felt; what discouraged me was the prospect of hearing the truth myself. It was as if those feelings wouldn't exist unless I heard myself talk about them—they would become real only when I said their names. I kept quiet about many things because of that fear, I suppose.

She cooked incredibly delicious dishes.

We didn't go to the studio for eleven days. And I didn't go to school. When we weren't making love we would either watch a documentary or go for a walk until we became hungry, eating at any restaurant we came across. She was always the one to pay the bill.

The relationship she had with money was uncharted territory for me. It worried me and at times it even made me furious. One day while strolling around we spotted an adjustable floor lamp in the window of an antique store. It was in the old style, with a small brass ball at the end of the chain attached to its column. When you pulled the ball, the lampshade turned downward. It gave a beautiful light, soft and smooth. The shade moving up and down with the pulling of the ball made the lamp's amber light open and close like primrose blossoms.

She walked into the store at once. And I followed her.

"How much is that lamp?" she asked.

"Seven thousand liras," said the man.

Without even asking for a better price she said, "I'm buying it, please wrap it well, I don't want it to break on the way home." I was amazed. We were being paid seventy liras per

day at the studio. Hayat Hanım had just spent a hundred days'
pay on a whim. I took the tightly wrapped lamp. Having gone
through penniless days recently I thought what she had done
was irresponsible.

"You just spent what you make in a hundred days on a
lamp," I said.

"On what should I spend what I make in a hundred days?"

"I don't know... To me this feels a bit irresponsible."

"Irresponsible to whom?"

"To yourself."

"What is my responsibility to myself?"

"To keep yourself safe and secure."

"Is that my only responsibility?"

"Your primary one."

"Is that what they taught you?"

"Yes."

"Oh, well."

She didn't say anything else. I couldn't bear the argument
ending like that.

"Isn't that so?" I asked.

"Perhaps it isn't."

"What is it, then?"

"You mean what's my responsibility to myself?"

"Yes."

She looked at me and laughed.

"Perhaps I don't have a responsibility to myself. Or maybe
my responsibility is to make myself happy. Just as I'm trying
to do now, and you're trying to ruin it for me..."

"Does a lamp make you happy?"

"Yes...Very much so."

"What happens if you need that money for something else tomorrow?"

"What if I don't need that money for something else tomorrow?"

"You will still be safe."

"What if I enjoy being happy more than I enjoy being safe..."

I knew I was playing the part of the nerdy idiot in this conversation, but I couldn't let it go.

"You may regret this purchase tomorrow."

"Had I not purchased it today I would have regretted it already."

At that moment we passed a street florist. She saw mimosas. She bought a big bunch of them as if we hadn't just had that conversation. When we arrived at her place, she immediately moved away the old lamp that was near the sofa, put the new one there, and turned it on. She put the yellow mimosas in the vase on the dining table. It had begun to rain—droplets were flowing down the window, and the lamp's amber light was falling on the droplets on the window and on Hayat Hanım's ginger-gold hair.

She looked at the light and laughed joyfully.

"I feel like Cleopatra," she said.

I didn't get it.

"What's this got to do with Cleopatra?"

She came and kissed me.

"I don't know, Mark Antony," she said.

I was an idiot, and worse still I was the one who was now regretful, I felt I had acted senselessly. She went inside, singing happily. A song I had never heard before: "Love likes chance encounters / Fate likes separation / Years like to pass / People like to seek." She came back in the short dress that revealed her bare breasts and the full swing of her hips.

"Come on," she said, "help me prepare dinner."

I kept touching her in the kitchen, rubbing myself against her without a word.

"What do you want?" she asked.

I just looked at her face.

"You don't deserve it," she said, "but so be it."

After we had made love and were eating dinner, she spoke as if in an effort to console me: "I didn't pay that money for the lamp, I paid for its light." She seemed confident that this was a perfectly reasonable explanation. I couldn't help laughing; sometimes I felt like I was her son and at other times, like at that moment, I felt like I was her father; in either case, of the two of us she was the more interesting one. I would always follow her with a bit of delay, feeling somewhat bemused all the time.

When we finished eating we took our coffees and sat in front of the TV. She plopped into her armchair with her feet tucked under her and skirt slipping up all the way. I was staring at her, and at that moment I thought I saw a side of her that I hadn't noticed before: her singular loneliness. She had retreated into a solitude that was only hers, one that amused her, made her happy even, and she had forgotten about me. Afterward, I would watch her retreat into that solitary place again and again, always with a self-satisfied smile on her face. Whenever I said something she would emerge from that solitude with the same natural quiescence she had when she withdrew herself. Loneliness was her nest. Like a bird with beautiful wings she could breeze in and out of that nest with ease. This was a habit I hadn't seen in anyone else. Her loneliness dazzled me, making me wish to enter that solitary place too. I wanted to have a solitude that belonged to the two of us.

There was a documentary about ants on TV. For the first time in my life I was watching something that was as captivating as literature. Different species of ants had various, rather bewildering qualities. A desert-dwelling ant looked exactly like an astronaut—they had invented their own special space suits millions of years before humans did and wore them while they lived on the dunes.

Blind ants built underground cities that had streets, avenues, and compounds with chambers. They developed special systems for air-conditioning and took precautions against flooding. And the same species of ants anywhere in the world built the same type of cities. Leaf ants burst into song when they found a high-quality leaf. They ventriloquized the song, their voice passing from their tiny legs to leaves and spreading the sound around so that the porter ants, tasked with carrying leaves to the nest, could hear it and come at once. Ants who conspired and campaigned for a palace coup to overthrow the queen ant would eat her if they managed to bring her down.

Now I understood why Maeterlinck had taken the time to write, beside his poetry, a book on ants. I regretted not having read the book and decided to look for it where they sold secondhand books. For the first time I was discovering a world outside literature that was similarly colorful.

When the documentary was over, Hayat Hanım asked me if I liked it. "I did," I said. "It never occurred to me that ants could be capable of a palace coup."

"Monkeys have such political fights too! Those who want to be elected president distribute bananas to others in exchange for votes, they go on campaign trips, they hug and stroke babies on the road."

She got up.

"Should we have another coffee before we go to bed?"

"Sure."

I followed her to the kitchen, and she laughed. "Don't worry, we're going to bed soon." As we drank our coffee, I asked her how she got the idea of becoming an extra on that TV show.

"I had a friend who was friends with the owner of that channel. He asked me if I'd like to go there and said I'd enjoy it, and I said *why not*. I really enjoy myself there. The place is like an underground documentary: you witness people and events there that you'd never see anywhere else. It is like watching the adventures of a different species—plus you can take part in them."

I was looking at her legs.

"Let's go to bed," she said with a grin, "you're getting impatient."

With her I felt the magnificent pleasure of being a man, I learned to swim in a volcanic lava that smelled of lilies. I was on a safari of unending gratification. She enveloped me in her warm and natural sensuality, took me to foreign lands, taught me unknown sensations with her ease at touching. She showed me the way to feeling different kinds of desire.

As days passed I discovered new feelings, new ideas, a new sense of time, and a new way of living. When I touched her, time shifted into some other form; she used her *presence* in this world like a sharp knife to peel the time with, to get rid of the past and the future and allow the *now*, only that delicious core of the fruit, to emerge. The *here* and *now*, compressed under the thick layers of past and future and thus never felt or lived properly, were unchained when I was with her. The present moment, the very essence of time, was liberated from the past and the future and became my entire life. Memories of bygone years and the anxiety of those that are yet to come were erased. All of life was transformed into an infinite moment. Hayat Hanım pervaded that long unbroken moment with her joyous nonchalance, her teasing, her compassionate poise, and her inexhaustible lust. When I touched her, the past and the future ceased to exist; we were connected to life through a single moment infused with her *being*.

Discarding the past and the future granted me a magnificent sense of freedom. Hayat Hanım was free. She wasn't free through submission or defiance, she was free because she didn't care and because she didn't demand. When I touched her that sense of freedom engulfed me too. Only in that emancipated state was I able to get a real taste of life, and I soon became addicted to it. When I couldn't touch her the wings of time closed, the past and the future crushed the *moment* and clamped me down.

Hayat Hanım didn't mind anything, she didn't care a whit; nothing could hurt her. One night we went to a small tavern. At the next table there was a group of young people. One of the girls in the group, whether in a deliberate attempt to infuriate Hayat Hanım or just being a chatty drunk, asked her: "Is he your son?" I was worried Hayat Hanım could be offended by that question, but she just shook her hair and laughed. "Yes," she said. "And he is kind of a pain."

On the way back I said: "So now I am your son, eh, Mommy!"

"But you are a bit of a mischief!"

I told her about Oedipus.

"You are Oedipus now, is that so?"

"They call relationships like this Oedipal."

This cracked her up.

"Do you name relationships as if they were kittens?" she remarked. "Do you fear you would misplace them if you didn't have a proper name for them?"

We were a good couple: husband and wife, mother and son, queen and guard, prince and concubine—no matter what others saw in us, I knew we didn't fit their mold. With the paucity of information we had about life, with such a variety of resources, it was impossible for us to fit in any singular role. When she told me about nature, the universe, animals, and stars, I listened to her like an illiterate child. And when I told her about writers and philosophers, she listened to me like an ignorant child. She wasn't interested in literature, but when I talked about the lives of writers and philosophers I noticed she took an interest in them; she would listen to me then with the same kind of attention she gave to a documentary on ants.

"Kierkegaard was in love with a girl named Regina; he proposed to her and she accepted. But at the last moment Kierkegaard decided that he was too pessimistic and pious for marriage, so he left. Regina begged him to go back to her; she cried and moaned, but Kierkegaard didn't return."

"What happened afterward?"

"Regina married someone else and found happiness. Kierkegaard lived in misery all his life."

She looked at me.

"What a moron!" she said.

I raised a laugh. Not even Nermin Hanım would dare to call Kierkegaard a moron.

We made each other laugh all the time. I couldn't imagine having that much fun with anyone else. Our personalities, dispositions, educational backgrounds, likes, and dislikes were completely different, but there was an almost magical ease to our intimacy.

We talked a lot, although she never talked about herself. I didn't know anything about her past. Nor her future plans, nor the details of her present situation. She wouldn't talk to me about these things, and whenever I asked a question she would shrug and change the subject with a mere "There is nothing to tell." She was like a mystical galaxy that had entered my life. I could see her stars, her light, her brightness, her colors but I couldn't solve the mystery behind it all. I couldn't figure whether there was a secret buried in her past or merely that she had discovered being discreet made her even more charming. Perhaps talking about herself simply bored her. There was a dark place on the other side of all that gleam, but I could never penetrate that self-indulgent obscurity of hers, that black well of decadence that made her so very alluring.

Sometimes I tried to solve her as a puzzle, outfox her with my own cunning ways. Kaan Bey once told us in class that in order to know a person one should know their dreams. One night in bed I asked Hayat Hanım: "What's your wildest dream?" She giggled. Her laugh made me imagine pieces of diamonds colliding on black velvet.

"To travel faster than light," she said.

I was somewhat offended by her answer.

"I asked a serious question."

She sat up in bed, naked, her legs crossed, her full breasts slightly drooping forward, her limbs, her shoulders, and the tips of her light-brown pubic hair gilded in the subtle beams of the night lamp.

"Since I was a child I have dreamed of traveling faster than light," she said. "Think about it, if you are faster than light, you arrive at your destination before the ones there can see you. You are there with them, but for those who were there before you, you aren't there. Light follows from behind, carrying your image. And they think that image, which is not *you*, is you…Alas, it is a mere image. They ask your image something, and the invisible you answers. You and your image are two things apart from each other…It would have been so much fun to travel faster than light. Real people would be invisible, but visible people would be virtual."

She brought her face closer to mine. "What do you think? Could any other dream be more marvelous than that?"

I put my arms around her and pulled her toward me. "No, it couldn't," I said.

One sunny morning when we were having breakfast, she said: "It's so nice outside, let's go to the woods. I'll prepare something to eat and we can have a picnic."

She had sudden urges like that. She would have a flash of thought, out of the blue, and want to do something about it right away. She believed she could do anything she wanted, and she did so.

"How are we going to get there?"

"By car."

"Which car?"

"My car."

"Do you *have* a car?"

"I had bought one, but I don't like driving, so it just sits there in front of the house. You know how to drive, don't you?"

"I do."

"Good. You drive, then."

It was peaceful in the woods. We parked the car and walked among the trees. Dry leaves crackled under our feet. Leaves were reddening, and the sun shone through them, its rays illuminating the path ahead of us like a piece of gilt lacework. The cooling effect of tree trunks made the heat bearable, sweet. Light and shade played musical chairs. We came to a small opening and stopped, putting down our blanket. We sat down, and before long she lay on her back, putting her hands under her head and closing her eyes. I was watching her. There was a mild breeze, and the light on her moved when the leaves wiggled, sending gleaming ripples across her body.

She seemed to have forgotten about me once again. I was thinking about her, but I had no idea what she was thinking about. I knew I'd never be able to find out, and that bothered me. With a sense of resentment brewing deep down, I thought being unable to know what was on another person's mind was a huge vulnerability.

She opened her eyes abruptly with a happy expression on her face.

"Are you hungry?" she asked.

"A little."

She sat up, leaning on one arm, pulled the basket of sandwiches near her, took out paper plates and cups. We ate in silence. The only sound was the gentle rustling of the leaves.

"Could happiness be something like this?"

I didn't answer, and she didn't expect me to.

I never knew if I was happy with her, not until I received that fateful letter she wrote me. We didn't use to talk about our feelings. Once we were eating happily in a cozy local pub while a torrential rain pounded its windows, and I couldn't help asking her: "Are you happy?" She looked at me for a long time with an intensity that made me nervous. "You shouldn't ask a woman this question," she said, finally. "She might not know if she is happy or not, yet she might very well know what is lacking in her life. You shouldn't remind her of that." How could I have known that even the bravest of women worried over that lack...

After eating in silence, she lay down again, watching the leaves and the light dallying in between them. I put my hand on her leg. She winked at me and smiled.

"What's up?"

"Should we do it?"

"Do you really want it that much?

"Yes."

She checked the ground by feeling the blanket, then stood up. She pulled up her skirt, turned her back to me, and put her hands on a tree. It was very quick, three or four minutes altogether, but in that deserted place the mix of desire and fear culminated in such an elation that I felt my body break apart with it. I had never known such intense pleasure, sharp like broken glass, bleeding.

Only as I was buckling my belt did I grasp the risk in what we had done. We had no idea what could have happened if anyone in those woods had seen us doing what we did. Anything could have happened. Still, Hayat Hanım wasn't the slightest bit concerned. She was fearless. Whenever I talked about a possible menace, she always said, "At the very most we die." *At the very most we die.*

That night in bed she spoke with a sober voice I had not heard from her before: "One day you will forget everything about these days." Then she took a deep breath.

"I would like you to pick a moment, a single moment...And never forget that moment. If you try to keep everything in mind, you will forget it all. But if you pick a single moment, you can own it forever, you can always remember it...It would make me happy to think that a single moment about me will stay alive somewhere in your mind for as long as you live."

All she wanted was a single moment.

I was about to tell her that I'd remember more than a single moment, but she gently pressed her finger against my lips.

"Don't say anything," she said.

I didn't.

I fell asleep with an unusual sense of bliss and, mixed in that, a good dose of equally inexplicable sadness.

The next morning she was quieter than usual. She had her breakfast without saying much. She had not put on her short housedress, she was wearing a gray knee-length skirt. "You've neglected both school and work for quite a while now, time to go back to your routine..." she said after breakfast. "You go get some rest, and so will I."

She was sending me away. I felt blood rush to my face. I had never been humiliated like this. Without a word I walked to the door.

"Take this with you," I heard her say.

I turned. She was holding out the car key.

"You can drive it for a while, I never do anyway."

I thought of rejecting her offer with some harsh words, but it occurred to me that the key could be a sign that we could continue our affair. I couldn't risk cutting off the link between us. As I opened the door she called after me: "Are you leaving without giving me a kiss?" I turned and kissed her cheek coldly.

When I got into the car Nietzsche's phrase was resonating in my mind.

"Bitter is even the sweetest woman."

Such a bitter taste, it was burning me inside.

5

I was woken by noise before daybreak, but I was so exhausted that I went back to sleep immediately. When I got up I walked down to the kitchen to have tea and found a lot of people hovering around the table in fervent conversation.

"What's going on?" I asked Bodyguard.

"Cops raided the building before dawn," he said. "They took the two guys who live on the first floor."

"Why?"

"They posted an article on Facebook."

"Is that a crime?"

The young man everyone called Poet heard me and spoke between his teeth as he nervously rose to leave: "It is a crime if you make a joke about the government. No more jokes!"

"Are you serious?" I asked.

"*They* are serious," he said.

It was as if we were sitting in the palm of a giant who, whenever he wanted, could make a fist and crush us in it. We realized that we could be blamed for doing things we always did; we could be arrested someday at dawn because of a quip, because of a simple thing we had said. The infinity of the emerging threat scared us. We dispersed quietly. I left the building and began to walk to the car.

What happened at the boardinghouse added to my distress. Emotions, so very turbid and unfamiliar, were piled up in me, one on top of another, and with the smallest jolt they spread out, became too large for me to hold them in, and began to tear me apart. Sometimes I felt like I was being torn to pieces by a pack of wild beasts. What hurt me most were the questions I had about Hayat Hanım.

Why had Hayat Hanım sent me away? What had I done wrong? Was she fed up with me? Was she seeing someone else?

That last question, especially, petrified me; no other thought or feeling could end the spasm it created. Weirdly obsessed, I wanted to know her whereabouts at all times; it seemed only if someone would tell me that *she is here now* I could relax a bit; if only I could place her in a setting firmly in my mind then I could come out of that rigor. Whenever I couldn't place her within boundaries of a defined space, she slipped away from me, disappearing in a cloud of smoke only to emerge now and then all naked and laughing, and then to become invisible again in the fumes. Obscurity was the hotbed, the womb, where one's imagination, handicapped by a variety of *what-ifs*, gave birth to suspicions.

My inability to reach her whenever I wanted, this great source of despair, made my jealousy masquerade at times in various disguises of anxiety. I was afraid that something bad might happen to her, that she might die, or even worse she would be killed in one of her daring acts of madness. The disabled offspring of an imagination inseminated by obscurity was growing up and suffocating me. Sometimes, exhaustion made me feel empty inside, made all my emotions disappear. In those moments, I found myself in a state of peaceful fatigue. I didn't know how to cope with all of that. And I never learned how. With time, like a chronic patient, I got used to occasional attacks—although the pain I felt never subsided, I managed to overcome the anxiety it caused. The fact that I lost and found her many times before that ultimate incident also had a role in easing my anxiety.

I got into the driver seat. It was a nice small car. I liked the idea of having a vehicle, even though it didn't belong to me. My father had obstinately refused to buy me a car. "One has to own a car only when he himself can afford it," he used to say. I think he was obsessed with the idea that rich kids die in car crashes, and even my mom's intervention on my behalf couldn't make him change his position on that. As a rich boy I could never drive to school, and now, as a poor man, I was doing just that. It was chilly outside, but nonetheless I rolled down the window and put my elbow on the doorframe.

I had Kaan Bey's class that day. He had a low-pitched voice, one that you wouldn't expect from his diminutive figure. First he asked a question:

"Why did most writers who sought to bring change to their craft, to make it anew, do so by changing the style of their writing? Why did they find the idea of a new form more appealing than the idea of changing the essence of what they wrote?"

His eyes raked over the entire class, and then, as always, he answered his own question:

"Because the essence doesn't change."

He walked between our desks and kept speaking in a melancholy voice as if something troubled him:

"The essence of literature is people... People's feelings. And the seed from which all feelings germinate is the desire to possess. When you desire to possess another person, to own their soul, that is love. When you desire to own someone else's body, that is lust. When you desire to possess the kind of ability to scare other people and intimidate them into submission, that is power. When you desire to possess money, that is greed. When you desire immortality, to have the right to live after death, that is faith. Literature talks about and is sustained by these five main vessels, which all originate from the same mother lode—the desire to own. That is the *essence*."

He stopped and looked at the class.

"How will you change the *essence*? That is the question."

A sudden smile emerged in his grizzled beard.

"This term, I will be expecting from each one of you a comprehensive response to this question... Or you can counter my argument by developing and substantiating with examples your own thesis. Give it a think. And don't forget—your ability to debunk my argument successfully is worth more to me than your subscribing to it."

I left the classroom pondering: *I don't want to possess Hayat Hanım. I want to be with her.* Alas, there was something in that thought that wasn't altogether persuasive. I felt I was giving the wrong answer to a question. There was a precious doubt in my mind about my own way of thinking. *Perhaps I do want to possess her,* a voice spoke from within. What part of her did I desire to possess? Her body? *Yes,* someone else seemed to answer that question, *yes, I want to possess her body. What about her soul?* I didn't want to answer that question, I didn't even want to ask it. Alas, I couldn't get rid of it, it stuck in my mind. When I said *her soul,* I imagined her in the solitary place she retreated to whenever she watched TV, as if her solitude was her soul. I didn't know why I felt that way but I knew I wanted to make some space for myself within that solitude. Was this a desire to possess her, was it that same greed in disguise? Potential answers to these questions terrified me, because surely I was under the spell of that quiet and perplexing solitude...

That night Hayat Hanım didn't come. Sıla wasn't there either. I had no one I could talk to, everyone had left me. I was looking straight at the stage with empty eyes. A woman in an obscenely short skirt was singing. She had gorgeous legs. I remembered what Hayat Hanım once had said: "Women know what part of their body to reveal." There was something awkward about the woman's face, although I couldn't figure out what it was. I held her face in my gaze trying to understand what it was that looked so off. Then I realized at once: She didn't have lips. Her mouth was a mere cut. A defect one wouldn't expect to make any face attractive, but curiously it was the case here—her face was strikingly beautiful.

Afterward a male singer came on the stage along with three belly dancers dressed in sequined bustiers and slit skirts, their midriffs completely exposed. They danced with an unusual litheness.

During the intermission I went out to the corridor and bought a tea. Most women there were Hayat Hanım's age, and they were all blonde. Again, I remembered something Hayat Hanım had said. "No matter how they were born all women die blonde," she said once, laughing. I asked *why*. She told me women's facial lines became deeper as they aged, and dark hair color accentuated those wrinkles while lighter shades softened the look. And then she teased me, "Don't they tell you about these things in those books, Antony?"

I missed her.

I saw a few new faces among the women. Unlike others in the audience, they sat quietly, looking sorrowful almost, glancing around self-consciously, bewildered. They didn't belong there. If you looked at their faces closely enough you could see traces of hauteur.

In the second half, a clarion player did an improvised solo in the middle of a ballad; he played it like jazz. I'd have never imagined that a jazz sound could be produced in that place, and with a clarion no less. The man impressed me with his talent. Those seductive blonde women and the lecherous men eyeing them also appreciated what they heard.

When the night's session was over, I left after everyone else. I didn't want to rush. I walked alone in the streets. Arriving at the boardinghouse I first went up to the kitchen to see if anyone was around. It was deserted. I poured myself some tea and took my time in case someone came in. No one did. I went upstairs to my room. I went out on the balcony. I began to watch the neighborhood. The crowd seemed thinner than usual.

I went back in. The farmers were on their way to a dance. They would forever be going to that dance.

I didn't undress. Oddly, I was worried that undressing could make me even more vulnerable, lonelier. I sat on the bed with my clothes on. I fell asleep in them. I woke up early in the morning. The room was cramped. Airless. I went out in panic. I wandered on the streets. People were on their way to work. They, all of them, had sullen faces.

Toward noon I finally gathered enough courage to call Sıla.

"How are you?" I asked.

"I'm good. How are you?"

She sounded happy to hear my voice.

"What are you doing?"

"I found Saramago's *The Stone Raft* in Hakan's library. I'm reading it."

"Poor Pedro Orce," I said.

"Poor Pedro Orce," she said.

The scene where two women with lovers of their own had sex with Pedro Orce because they took pity on him for being lonely had very much impressed and made me think about one's goodness of heart.

There were very few people in this world who could respond to my *poor Pedro Orce* with their own *poor Pedro Orce*. I had found one of those people but had not appreciated her.

While reading *The Divine Comedy* I was very much touched by the story of Paolo and Francesca, whom Dante met in Hell; they had fallen in love while reading a book about love, defied all rules, and agreed to go to Hell. I had always dreamed of a love like that; falling in love with a woman while reading a book together. For me that was the greatest love possible. Our *poor Pedro Orce* exchange reminded me of that fantasy.

"You weren't there last night," I said.

"My class ended late, I couldn't make it," she said. "And you've been a no-show for quite some time."

"I wasn't here. My mom got sick, I went to see her, but she's fine now," I said. Because I didn't dare to suggest a date, I used Shakespeare as my disguise. "When shall we two meet again? In thunder, lighting, or in rain?"

I heard her laugh.

"We don't need to wait for such drama, we can just meet under an overcast sky."

"When will you be ready? What time should I pick you up? A friend of mine has lent me their car."

"I'll be ready in two hours."

I picked her up and drove to the shore. The sky was overcast. The sea had a grayish hue.

"Should we find a little restaurant to eat fish?"

"It will be too expensive."

"Who cares... I haven't used up my earnings from the TV program, I have some money. We can spend it on a meal."

"That would be irresponsible."

"Irresponsible to whom?"

"Irresponsible to yourself."

"Is that what they taught you?"

Hearing my own words bewildered me. Like the sea creatures in those deep-ocean documentaries, I was shape-shifting according to whomever I was with.

"That is what they taught me," said Sıla in a cold voice. "How did they teach *you*?"

"Fine. What should we do?"

"Let's stop by one of those teahouses on the shore. We can buy tea and grilled cheese sandwiches and eat them in the car."

We did as she suggested. While eating her sandwich she asked in her flattest voice: "Who was that woman?"

"Which woman?"

"The one we saw at the studio that evening."

"Oh, her! I have known her since my childhood. She is the sister of my mom's old seamstress."

I had learned to lie pretty quickly. It embarrassed me. Either I was disintegrating really fast, or my already-rotten core was simply revealing itself now that circumstances had changed. As if I, too, had changed when they altered the stage backdrop behind me.

The sea was flowing before us.

"Open the window," she said. "Let the sea breeze in... I adore the smell of the sea."

I opened the window.

"What do you think of those two women making love to Pedro Orce?" I asked.

She thought for a while, puckering her lips.

"Do you remember the woman breastfeeding the starving man in *The Grapes of Wrath*?"

"Yes."

"I think it's the same thing... They have something that can help a desperate person, and they give it to him. I think that's what being good is all about. Unforgettable scenes, both of them."

I couldn't hold back. "What wonderful bodies you have," I said, "feeding the hungry, comforting the lonely." She gave me a reproachful look, like a devotee rebuking someone for deriding her sacred truths. I immediately changed the subject.

"I saw new people at the studio," I said. "People unlike the usual crowd."

"I used to know some of them," she said.

"Did you really?"

"Yes. They are the wives of businessmen who have been sent to jail or whose assets have been taken away."

She continued with an uneasy voice: "It is as if someone is making all of us gather there... What are they going to do? Are they going to burn us all one night?"

"Oh, come on!" I said.

"I am exaggerating, but I do find it very unsettling. I'm going to quit that job. I ran into one of my former professors the other day; he's looking for a researcher to help with a book he wants to write. He asked me if I would do it."

"Does he know your father's situation?"

"I told him. He said, 'I don't care about such things. I am too old to be afraid.'"

"Will you accept his offer?"

"I will. That place isn't right for me anyway."

I was relieved to hear that Sıla wasn't coming back to the studio. The idea of her and Hayat Hanım being in the same room made me uneasy.

"It's better for you to do the kind of work you enjoy," I said.

It began to rain.

"Close the window," she said. "I'm a bit cold."

I rolled up the window.

"Should we have another tea?" I asked.

"That would be nice. It's pretty here...I miss looking at the sea."

For a while we sat quietly, drinking our tea, watching the water.

"What is your biggest dream?" I asked.

She puckered her lips, became pensive.

"To live a secure life... This is my biggest dream at the moment, my only dream, even. I don't know what my future dreams might be."

Then she asked me.

"What is your biggest dream?"

"To teach at the university... To teach literature."

"Yours is easier to achieve."

"Yes...But I really want to do it. Do you know Nermin Hanım and Kaan Bey?"

"I don't. But I've heard of them."

"Nermin Hanım has a class tomorrow morning, should we go together? I'd like you to see her teach."

"OK," she said. "I don't have class tomorrow, I'll go with you."

I was so happy to hear that. I was surprised by how happy it made me feel.

The rain began coming down harder. A strong, special bond had formed between Sıla and I, a connection that was built by the similarity in our tastes and backgrounds, our love of literature, and most important, the misfortune that befell both of us. Yet we didn't know what to do with that bond—we couldn't decide whether to remain friends or to become confidants or even lovers. A hesitation that must have resulted from our emotional ambivalence toward each other. Later, when I said to her, *It took us a long time to decide to become a couple*, she passed over my remark. *What was difficult wasn't to make the decision to become a couple*, she said. *The difficulty was in deciding whether to do it in a boardinghouse room.* I was taken aback by her calculated approach, which betrayed an indifference to instant urges, an ability to ignore desire and lust. Alas, this universe, which is woven with streaks of rebellious neurons that we call feelings, is quite bizarre. Her calculatedness, as unnerving as it was, also had a strong pull on me. I wanted to break that hard shell of circumspection and see what was inside. Who knows, I thought, I might find in there that scintillating sense of warmth I felt when our arms touched, a warmness that would in time become more profound by our mutual love for literature and suffice to make me happy. At times, when I least expected it, with a single word or a look or a touch and, sometimes, with a tear in her eye, she allowed me a glance at the soft and sweet core she nursed under that hard surface...and those brief moments kept my dream alive.

On the way back I asked her: "Tell me what would be the first thing you would do if you had money again?"

She answered at once: "I'd buy some perfume."

"Perfume?"

"Perfume...I feel incomplete without the scent I'm used to."

She said this like a little girl repeating what she had heard from her mother.

I dropped her off at her apartment and drove back. I parked on a backstreet. I bought a half loaf, some cheese, and a can of beer in a grocery store on the way to the boardinghouse and went up to my room. That suffocating sense of loneliness had been lifted. I missed Hayat Hanım, but I also enjoyed hanging out with Sıla. They were so unlike each other. Indeed, they were two completely opposite characters. I remembered what Nermin Hanım said: "One should avoid sharp contrasts in a work of literature. Stark opposites cheapen the work...If you want to have characters that are complete opposites of each other, then you should use the contrast between them in a complementary manner, in order to form a whole."

Knowing I would meet with Sıla in the morning gave me a sense of peace and safety. I appreciated what a gift it was to be able to go to bed knowing one would be able to talk to someone the next day. I was wondering where Hayat Hanım was, but my longing and concern for her had eased a bit since the day before. My feelings changed rapidly. I resembled a building whose foundation had cracked in a major quake, I thought, so that things in that building were no longer safe and reliable. I could hear the crackling noises inside me.

I stepped out onto the balcony and looked at the street. The familiar crowd was gone. Every day there were fewer people on the street now, it seemed. I undressed and went to bed.

I left without eating breakfast in the morning. Sıla got in the car, holding a paper bag: "I've got pastries!" We drove to school, quietly, eating our hot cheese-filled buns. She was exquisite. Like a really good novel, her beauty kept me on my toes, pulling me in continuously. I felt grateful for it.

The classroom was packed, as always. We sat side by side in the back row. When Nermin Hanım walked in, Sıla leaned to whisper in my ear. "Her shoes are *très chic*," she said.

Nermin Hanım talked, all the while clacking the temples of her reading glasses as if they were a pair of castanets:

"Writers are like animals who can hear sounds humans can't hear and smell odors humans can't smell. They can sense all kinds of emotions, shapeless, nameless desires, which settle in that dark place we call the subconscious—things that remain beyond other people's perception. However, those writers, the very same, fail in return at grasping some facts that others can easily see or smell, or feel at their fingertips."

She shot the classroom a glance.

"Clear and solid facts have a hard time finding their way into the convoluted minds of writers . . . This strange conflict changes reality, it alters the entire human existence. We see in literature, through the lens of writers, what we fail to take stock of in our own lives. And considering what a failure they themselves are at living an ordinary life, we forgive writers for the power they hold over us, the source not only of our admiration but also our secret resentment of them. Writers' biographies appeal to us so deeply, for they reveal this pathetic conflict; they let the reader forgive the writer, help us cultivate a sense of superiority over him."

She sat on the rostrum and crossed her legs.

"Baudelaire's poem 'The Albatross' is a fine example of this conflict… This vast winged bird for all its glory in the sky becomes equally awkward and weak once it lands on the planks of a ship."

After class I asked Sıla if she wanted to have a bite at the cafeteria. "It will be expensive," she said. I couldn't quite understand the reason behind her frequent emphasis on being on a budget—was this her way of taking revenge or was it simply out of the despair she felt at being penniless?

I didn't want to leave her yet. There was no session at the studio, and the idea of spending the evening alone terrified me.

"Should we go to the movies?" I asked.

"To the movies?"

"Yes."

After a moment of hesitation, she said, "OK," as if giving license to reckless extravagance. "I haven't been to a movie theater for so long."

On the way I asked her: "How did you like Nermin Hanım?"

"Good lecturer," she said. "She is so grandiose, though, as if she's above all those writers she lectures on. Still, she knows to add allure to arrogance. When I go home I'll reread 'The Albatross' on the web."

We decided to go to a movie theater in a shopping mall. Sıla zoomed up the escalator all the way to the top floor without glancing at a single shopwindow. I followed her, bewildered by her speed.

"Which movie should we see?" I asked.

"Whatever... There's nothing I especially want to see... Get tickets for the movie that starts the soonest, let's take a chance."

I bought two student tickets. When the movie began she took out a pair of glasses from her purse and put them on. I hadn't seen her with glasses before. It was an action movie. She watched it intensely, her arm touching mine. Every now and then I turned to look at her.

During the intermission I asked if I should buy popcorn. "If it won't be too irresponsible, that is..."

She took off her glasses and stared at me. "Don't piss me off, now!"

We were the same age, we came from similar families, we went to similar schools, we read similar books, and there was no way on earth I could say to anyone *Don't you piss me off, now!* as gracefully, as threateningly, and as attractively as she did. I wanted to lean over and kiss her. I felt shy around her, I didn't know why, but her sweetness and charm somehow intimidated me.

In the second half of the movie, she put her glasses back on. Now and again her arm brushed against mine. I didn't know whether she was conscious of that, but I was. Once the movie was over we took the escalators down, without rushing. The mall looked empty, with only a few people still around.

At the bottom of the escalators there was a famous candy store. The shop's window gleamed like a jeweler's display case. Sıla stopped and began looking at the truffles in the window. Candied orange peels covered in chocolate; *marrons déguisés*, with green tops dipped in finely ground pistachios; chocolate medallions; pralines in the form of seashells; cherry fondants wrapped in shiny red paper; chocolate-covered raisins scattered on the tray like black pearls...

"Which one is your favorite?" I asked.

"I like them all," she said, "but mostly the ones with orange, perhaps."

"Should we buy a hundred grams?"

She didn't respond.

As I was entering the store she called from behind me: "Get two pieces of *marrons déguisés* as well."

I went in and asked a salesperson clad in a deep red-and-navy apron for a hundred grams of chocolate orange truffles. The man took a small brown paper bag out from under the fancy chocolate boxes, slipped on a sheer glove, and began putting the truffles in. While he weighed the bag I asked: "May I also have two *marrons déguisés*?"

He gave me a pitiful look and put the two truffles in the bag. Outside the store, I gave the bag to Sıla. She held it with both hands. The smile of an exultant little girl appeared on her face—I had no idea she could smile like that. I'd never seen her that happy.

We went down to the parking garage under the mall and got in the car. With rows of concrete columns and, parked between them, cars that looked dark like sarcophagi under the gloomy lamps buried in the walls, the garage resembled a catacomb from prehistoric times. Just as I was about to turn on the engine I sensed something was off. I turned. She was crying.

"What happened?"

"Nothing," she said.

I got anxious. "What happened?" I asked again.

Suddenly, she began to sob. "I can't stand it sometimes," she said sobbing. "I can't stand that a hundred grams of chocolate is making me *so* happy."

I didn't know what to say. I kept quiet.

She wiped off her eyes and said: "I'm sorry, let's get out of here."

We left the parking garage. She handed me the paper bag.

"Thank you," I said. "You eat it. I'm not that keen on chocolate."

Her slender fingers dug out an orange truffle from the bag. She took a small bite. She chewed slowly, savoring it.

She offered me the bitten truffle.

"Try it," she said. "It's delicious."

I did. I hadn't eaten chocolate for quite a while. It really was delicious. She put the remaining morsel into her mouth and gently licked her fingertips.

Taking turns to eat the same truffle in small bites, a wonderful gesture of intimacy one could only perform with someone very close, felt to me like a secret act of lovemaking. As if I had seen her stark naked before me, I got turned on at once. Biting the same truffle was like an embrace that allowed us to feel the warmth hidden in the depths. I felt a strong desire for her, a longing that ached in my groin, as well as a starkly different kind of affection, one filled with tenderness. A single piece of chocolate had been enough to create in me an emotion akin to love.

I was looking at my lap.

In the past, such small gestures hadn't provoked major waves of emotion in me. As my loneliness expanded, so had my feelings—they were swollen and windswept like rain clouds in that vast solitude.

As we got close to where Sıla lived, I asked: "What are you doing tomorrow?"

"Tomorrow and the next day, I have classes. But I'm free after that."

"I'll call you," I said.

Before she got out of the car, she leaned toward me and kissed the edge of my mouth. I felt the warmth of her lips and the smell of chocolate.

6

I got up early in the morning, bought half a loaf at the corner store and had them put some *kashar* cheese in it. I went back in, walked up to the kitchen, took out a plate, put it on the table, and put my loaf on it. I was pouring myself some tea at the counter when I heard Gülsüm behind me.

"Whose loaf is that?"

I turned and looked at her, "It's mine," I said.

With her hip-hugging miniskirt, her lavender hoodie zipped down to her navel that left most of her bosom bare, her high heels in size eleven, her untidy black mane with a single lock of blond hair in the front, her slightly smudged mascara, which turned her eyes into round holes peering out of a purple mask, and her glossy lipstick smeared around her mouth, she stood in that century-old kitchen like a multicolored spaceship. As usual, her presence made me somewhat uneasy.

"Oh, damn," she said. "I thought someone had left it behind. I'm starving."

"Help yourself to half of it," I said. "Would you like some tea as well?"

"I sure would…"

She had broken the bread into two and was already eating her half when I brought the tea and sat across from her. While we both ate with appetite she began talking.

"I'm exhausted, we pulled an all-nighter, two blokes and me, they trashed me. Contractors! That's what they are. They've become contractors, recently. Those are the guys with dough these days. Tradesmen all went under. Anyhoo, those two smashed me all night."

Then she laughed.

"But…I was paid handsomely. I got bruised all over, but it was worth it. They *will* come calling again."

I smelled alcohol on her breath. She looked hungover. Despite the impudence of her language one could hear in her voice the pure joy of an innocent child of poverty who had just found a wad of cash on the street. Yet I had also seen on a few occasions that rare innocence of hers abruptly switch to an aggressive rudeness. Once she had brought a candy bar for Tevhide—she adored the little girl as much as the rest of us. Emir wanted to keep his little daughter away from sweets, and said that *Tevhide doesn't eat chocolate*, and all at once the charming auntie who'd brought candy to her niece turned into a bitchy bully. She turning on Emir, saying "Ain't I worthy of offering chocolate to your daughter?" Luckily, that unpleasant scene culminated in laughter, when Tevhide said, "Come on, Gülsüm, you fire up so easily."

"Can I ask you a question?" I said somewhat warily.

"Go ahead," she said. "Although it usually means trouble when someone begins with 'Can I ask you something?' What's up, tell me?"

What I really wanted to ask was what it was like to be both man and woman—two creatures that seek, desire, and are enamored with each other—in a single body. However, I feared that would be improper, and I asked another question, something that had just popped into my head.

"Why do men come to you rather than going to women?"

"Blokes prefer us," she said. "We know what they itch for, we blow their minds... They find in us something they can never find in broads."

To change the subject, I asked her what her biggest dream was. She leaned back and asked, "My biggest dream?"

"Yeah," I said.

She put her elbows on the table; her face became serious.

"To watch a derby game in the stadium."

"You mean, going to a football match?" I said in amazement. Suddenly she got angry.

"What's wrong?" she said. "Women go, don't they? Why shouldn't I?"

"Err, that's not what I meant," I mumbled.

"Isn't there someone you love, you dream about being with?"

She wrinkled her face—a woeful, angry grimace. "There's this one beast. He's a cook in a restaurant down the road. When he gets drunk and horny, it's 'Come here, Gülsüm...' He fucks me in the back of the restaurant until dawn. If I ask then whether he loves me, 'I love you so much, Gülsüm,' he says. Then once he's done, he doesn't call until he's horny again. With a hard-on everyone loves everyone else. Loving someone when you've got a softie, now *that* is manly. But where does one find a man like that? They all bend you over, first they fuck you and then they fuck off... You are the same, I bet. All of you."

I was learning a new language in the kitchen, one that was entirely foreign to me. In this language, words had different meanings.

"Why get riled up at me, dude? Why go apeshit on me?"

I said those words awkwardly, like a child just learning to talk. Gülsüm, however, was used to such talk, so she just heard what I said and didn't catch my awkwardness in using those words. Her hangover might also have helped.

She laughed.

"You're right, I suddenly got riled up. It happens when I talk about that brute of mine. I miss the beast but he drives me nuts."

We both took a bite of our loaves.

"What you do—isn't it dangerous?"

"Of course it's dangerous... Boy, is it ever. You get yourself under a completely unfamiliar man, you have no idea whether drifter or grifter, you have your back to the bloke, and if he decides to put a knife in you you won't even see it coming."

She finished her loaf and got up to leave.

"Thanks for the bread," she said. "I'm going to bed. I'm exhausted."

On her way out of the kitchen she ran into Poet, at whose sight I saw that drunken smirk erased from Gülsüm's face, replaced by the kind of respectful awe that one sees on the faces of people who encounter an older person they hold in high esteem. Poet patted her gently on the shoulder: "How are you, Gülsüm?"

"I am good, bro, I came back from work and am going to bed."

Walking toward the samovar, Poet said, "Up you go, sweet dreams." Then, adding with a grin:

"Are you still afraid of walking across the courtyard?"

Gülsüm looked down shyly. "I won't walk through there, bro, I'll be struck down."

"Someday, we should walk across together," said Poet.

Once Gülsüm left, Poet saw me looking at him curiously.

"You know the small mosque at the bottom of the street," he said.

"Yes."

"Everyone uses its courtyard as a shortcut, but Gülsüm can't bring herself to do that. Instead, she walks all the way to the square in order to get back up here. She believes God will smite her if she goes near that mosque; she thinks she has no right to get anywhere near it because she's a sinner."

I was baffled. "Is Gülsüm religious?"

"Why shouldn't she be? Doesn't she have the right to be religious?"

I was embarrassed. Poet laughed: "She believes God takes people seriously."

I laughed too. "Doesn't he?"

"Why would he take us seriously? God must have been regretting what he did for a long time now; he must be trying to put this all behind him. I'm sure he must have torn out our page from his scrapbook."

He drank up his tea, washed, and dried his glass with a towel.

"What happened to the guys the cops took away?"

"They were arrested."

"What were they accused of?"

"They'll certainly come up with some sort of a crime. A long list to choose from."

Walking to the door, he said, "Anyway...I need to go now, but let's find a good time to sit down and chat."

All I knew about people was whatever the novels managed to take out from under that fathomless cloak of humanity and reveal to us. People's images were illuminated for me only by the stark light of literature. Now that, for the first time ever, I could see people in my own mental glare without the help of any other lens, I was beginning to understand that I didn't really know them. It would have never occurred to me that Gülsüm's biggest dream could be to go to a soccer game. Yet what baffled me even more than that was Gülsüm's blaming herself—and not the Creator she believed to have made her—for the circumstances, all that suffering, the job she had to keep and the dangers she faced. A while later, when Gülsüm was hospitalized after a stabbing and Bodyguard and I went to visit her, we would discover that she held herself responsible for not only what befell her but also everything else that happened to people around her. She believed her loved ones were also being punished for her sins. She cried, wiping her tears with the edge of the muslin scarf she wrapped around her hair. I couldn't normally bring myself to touch her, but I held her hand that day, and said, "Don't be sad." Bodyguard, having a much clearer mind, one without the clutter of my conflicting ideas and emotions, spoke rather harshly but sounded much more like an equal than I had managed to: "You're tripping, Gülsüm." I loved people perhaps more than Bodyguard did, but amid my various opinions, judgments, and prejudices my affection faded somehow. It became complicated, less sincere.

One day during that time when we were getting closer and closer to a tragic event, we were at the pub across from the building, drinking to cheer up Gülsüm after some misfortune she had to deal with. "*I love people*—now, those are big words. One doesn't have to love people," said Poet. "But all of these desperate people, the people who are taken advantage of by the others, can join forces to come up with a solution."

Emir, who usually keeps to himself in such conversations, joined in unexpectedly, speaking with a calm voice. "History teaches us that now and again people intend to do just that, but they lack the willpower to carry it to the end. Whatever they do they always fall in the same snare of evil. That trap is always there. Show me a society, any society, that managed to be happy after the invention of agriculture."

I laughed. "Are you suggesting we go back to hunter-gatherer tribes?"

"If that were a choice, I'd vote for that."

Poet got serious and said, "Your class consciousness finds solace in escaping to the past in order to justify today's world order."

Emir responded in the same calm manner: "And your class consciousness tells you to escape to the future. At the end of the day, we're all trying to escape from the present. Some of us flee back, some of us flee forward because we can't come up with a solution for what's going on here and now."

"We're all on the run, I gather," I intervened. Tevhide, who seemed completely focused on her lamb chop, was suddenly intrigued: "On the run? Where to? I'll also run away, then." Poet patted Tevhide on the head: "Don't run away, Tevhide, darling. At least *you* should stay here."

Little did we know that we were speaking on the edge of an abyss. Still, each of us in our own way, we tried to hang on together. One of us would have to let go and fall, but we didn't know that yet. Poet told funny stories that made all of us chuckle. Tevhide laughed the most.

When I told Hayat Hanım about that conversation she began to talk without hesitation as if she had been thinking about the same issues: "People are able to change everything except themselves. That's our curse."

When I talked about it with Sıla, she reminded me about Kaan Bey's lecture: "How can people change without changing their desire to possess things? ... Doesn't literature tell us about the impasse created by our inability to change? *That* must be what Emir calls the snare of evil."

After Gülsüm and Poet had left I had another glass of tea in the kitchen and went out. It was a nice sunny day. There was a session at the studio that night, but Sıla wasn't going, and I didn't know whether Hayat Hanım would be there. I thought for some reason that if she didn't show up that night it meant she would never show up again.

I decided to go to the old booksellers' arcade to look for Maeterlinck's book *The Life of the Ant*. There was no one there. I looked into the shop where the shopkeeper had given me the photograph of the farmers. It was closed, its window plastered with old newspapers. Only three shops were open in the entire arcade. I went into one and asked for the book.

"It's been a long time since anyone asked for that book," said the shopkeeper, "they didn't reprint it. It's very hard to find. I'd find you one in the old days, but now we'll probably close the shop before I can spot it somewhere. They will tear this place down any day now."

I left. I used to enjoy being by myself, but now solitude bored me. I walked around. The whole city was tired of solitude, I thought. Toward the evening I went back to my room. For a while I read my dictionary of mythology. When gods wanted to save someone from something they just wrapped him in clouds and whisked him away. I wish they would whisk me away, or at least that my farmers would take me to the dance with them. I dozed off thinking about this. I woke up, worried I was late to the session, but there was still time. I walked to the studio.

The program had just started. As soon as I entered that illuminated darkness I surveyed the stage, Hayat Hanım was sitting in her usual place in her honey-colored dress. I felt the air rush to my lungs, as if I had been only half breathing until that moment. I sighed with joy. At one point her face came on the large screen, and soon after that I saw my own face there as well. A sad face, surprisingly so, when I thought I was filled with joy.

A short-haired singer wearing a yellow evening dress with black patterns was singing playful songs. Hayat Hanım was dancing with all the others, but she moved in a way that was more appealing and more jovial than the rest. Her body swung in harmony.

In the intermission she stepped off the platform and came straight to where I was sitting.

"How are you, Antony?"

"I'm good, thank you. How are you?"

"I'm fine. Let's get out of the hall."

We went into the corridor. It was crowded. We sat on two chairs, side by side.

"Don't disappear after the show, so we can have dinner together," she said.

"OK."

At that very moment a hush passed over the crowd. Everyone stopped talking, and retreated slightly to the walls. A man of medium height, with wide shoulders and a frown on his face, had come down the stairs. He was in a suit and was followed by two tall men in dark suits. When he walked by us he stopped to ask: "How are you doing, Hayat?"

"I'm fine. How are you?"

They had greeted each other with a special kind of distance, one that could only exist between people who were once very close, I thought. The friendly manner in which they addressed each other was in contrast to the remove in their voices, an odd discrepancy that could only belong to a relationship between people who had once been intimate with each other but who had later closed that book for good. I sensed this without knowing how I sensed it. To discern such things one didn't need to have experienced it, I suppose. Theirs was such a particular way of greeting, it was impossible not to notice.

They didn't say anything else to each other. The man and the men behind him passed us and walked away.

"Who is that man?" I asked.

Hayat Hanım responded in a chilling voice: "Stay away from him!"

I now understood who had secured this job for Hayat Hanım. I was filled with rage, an anger the cause and aim of which I couldn't pinpoint.

After the session, I waited for Hayat Hanım to change her outfit. Then we left together.

"I didn't drive here," I said, "the car is parked on a street near the boardinghouse. We can go get it if you'd like, or I can."

"Better to leave it there," she said. "It is going to be hard to find a parking place near my home at this time of night, better not to deal with all that."

After we walked for a while, she said: "We can eat at home if you'd like, I can make a few things. Or would you rather go to a restaurant?"

"Let's eat at home." My voice sounded somewhat sulky, almost resentful of Hayat Hanım.

We got in a cab. The lights of the large delicatessen at the bottom of the hill where Hayat Hanım lived were still on. She asked the driver to stop by the store. "Come on," she said, "let's buy a few things, that way we won't have to waste time cooking."

The man at the counter greeted us warmly.

"Welcome, Hayat Hanım. How are you?"

"Thank you. How come you're open this late?"

"I'm waiting for a delivery and kept the lights on just in case a customer would walk in."

"How's business?"

"Flat. Not like what it used to be. No one has money anymore. And those who still have some hold on to it tightly. Everyone is afraid of tomorrow."

Clearly, Hayat Hanım wasn't one to be afraid. Smoked tongue, Hungarian salami, cured pastrami, roast beef, Russian salad, pickles, hummus, stuffed mussels, and a bottle of good wine... She bought with appetite. I could barely carry the huge paper bag.

"We brought the man back to life," I said.

She looked at me quizzically.

"He said everyone is afraid of spending money, but you certainly aren't."

"I don't like being afraid, fears turn me off."

"Being broke is not all that easy, you know."

"I know what it's like to be broke, Antony. When one's got money one should live like one's got money! To have money and to live like you don't have any is as foolish as living like you have money when you don't. We'll think about it when we run out of money. We haven't yet, so let's enjoy ourselves."

"Wouldn't it be too late to think about it when the money is all gone? One can easily be driven from pillar to post."

We were at her door already. She gave me that sardonic smile of hers.

"Do you want me to be afraid?"

"Yes."

"Why?"

"It's good to be a little afraid."

She got serious. "Being afraid is never good."

Then, she smiled again. "You shouldn't be afraid either, Antony… There is nothing to be afraid of in this life. Life is good for one thing only: living. It would be stupid to postpone everything in an attempt to save up on life, like misers. You can't save up on life… Even if you don't spend it, it spends and consumes itself to the end."

When we were going up in the lift, she giggled. "You'll see what happens if the earth tilts now. This place will turn into a desert, and all money will become dust."

I could smell the scent of lilies on her. When we entered the apartment she told me to sit down. "I'll go and change."

She came back wearing her spaghetti-strap beach dress and black slippers. Looking at her breasts and thighs moving freely under the thin garment, I could see she was naked underneath. At once, I had forgotten about fear and money and earth. The provocative memories of our days together filled up my mind. Life was good for one thing only: living. And at that moment there was only one thing I wanted to do in order to feel alive, the one thing I could give up everything else for.

She saw the way I looked at her. "Aren't you hungry?" she asked.

"I can eat afterward."

That wry smile again, sardonic and self-satisfied...Her smile expanded and pulled me inside.

"All right, then."

She turned around and walked toward the bedroom.

The moment we embraced I knew how much I had missed her. There was nothing that was more thrilling, more gratifying for me than holding her in my arms and making love to her. When I hugged her and she pulled me closer, I, too, knew: *There is nothing to be afraid of, there is no need to be afraid.* She didn't need to tell me any of that—her embrace was enough to make me feel it.

Fear and worry, the past, and the future disappeared in her bosom, and only a radiant solitude and a sensual darkness remained. I grew up, aged, and matured in her bosom, and I didn't care about anything else. Just the same, as soon as I left her side my fears always came back, time expanded again, my anxiety and distress heightened. Still, after each time we were together, a drop of what I had done and felt in her company was added to a receptacle in my mind—a receptacle that belonged to Hayat Hanım only—and accumulated there like gold coins.

When we sat down for dinner it was past midnight. I was starving. The mezes were delicious. The room was infused with the soft amber light of the brass lamp. After I satisfied my hunger and had a little wine, I asked the question I'd been itching to ask for days.

"Why did you send me away?"

I saw, for the first time ever, a bewildered look on her face.

"I sent you *away*?"

"Didn't you? *Go, live your life a little.* What was that supposed to mean?"

She held my hand. "I never thought you'd take it the wrong way," she said, "I'm such a fool! You weren't going to school, you weren't going to work, the way it was going you'd soon believe you were jeopardizing your future and resent me for it. With such resentment you wouldn't want to have anything to do with me anymore... I didn't want you to be angry and fed up with me. I want you to think about me, *and only me*, when we're together, I want you to have nothing else on your mind, no worries whatsoever."

She paused. "Why didn't you ask me about this that morning?"

"Because I was furious."

She came and sat on my lap, kissed me on the lips. "Oh, Antony, you're so dumb." Then she got serious. "If something like that happens again, ask me before you make up your mind about it." She chuckled again, then she covered my face with her mane and brought her mouth to my ear: "And because you are so dumb, you draw the wrong conclusions and make the wrong decisions."

We cleared the dining table together. I was happy. As was the case with me lately, my feelings had changed on the spur of the moment. I was easily swayed from one end to the other. Like a ball of feathers, I was weightless.

And I was too proud to ask about the man we saw at the studio. Instead, I asked a more general question as we were drinking our coffee.

"What are your standards in men? What makes you fancy a man?"

"Standards? Rules? Are we talking about construction work? I just fancy some guys, that's all there is to it."

"Which guys?"

"I don't know. Never thought about it."

"You *never* thought about this?"

"I never did. Would you like another coffee?"

As we drank our second cup she turned on the TV. We watched the last few minutes of a documentary. It was about a luminescent millipede in the Amazon jungle. In the night, it moved like a glowing train on the steppes. Once it spotted an appetizing bug, it went all dark, and only after feasting on its prey did it turn its lights back on.

She got up from her chair to fetch something from the kitchen. I watched her from behind. Her skirt had bunched around her thighs. She didn't have her slippers on. She walked on tiptoe. I thought of a line from Hesiod, where he talks about goddesses with "petal-soft feet," under which "tender grass sprouted up." She reminded me of a wide heath, a heath that's as green as it can be, soft and beautiful, expanding all the way to the sun itself, nestled in and inseparable from a cosmic landscape: Her spontaneous inner joy, her libido, soft and green like leaves of grass moving with a never-ceasing breeze, and that nonchalance of hers, which gave everything she touched a brilliant levity...

Whatever she desired she desired with a passion: A lamp, to dance to a playful tune, me, a peach, to make love, a delicious meal...But I also knew that she could give up whatever she so fervidly desired with an ease equal in its strength to her passion. She acted not only with an assumed license to desire everything but also the power to let everything go. The inherent ceaselessness of her desires came from a conviction in her own ability to abandon them. Had she lost faith in her capability to let go of something, she wouldn't have desired it anymore.

On her way back to her chair, she took a piece of tangerine from the dining table and kissed me on my neck. Then, she put her feet under her and sat down, smiling. Just like that, she retreated into her solitary place. She closed her wings and went into her nest. Unaffected and calm, like an unhurried rain on a warm evening in springtime. For a second only, I wondered whether her fondness for documentaries was a result of her ways resembling the ways of nature more than those of her fellow humans.

I remembered what Nermin Hanım had said about writers: "Everyone knows the rules of literature, but only writers know how to violate those rules." Everyone knew the rules of living, even *I* did, but only Hayat Hanım knew how to violate those rules. She violated the rules with her innate spontaneity. The first rule of living was to be afraid, yet she wasn't afraid...Almost nothing scared her.

I looked at her. She was leaning over a bit, her breasts showing all the way to her nipples.

"What now, Antony?"

"Should we go to sleep?"

She was a goddess in bed. Like Hesiod's goddess Hecate, there was no blessing Hayat Hanım couldn't bestow on men. She did bestow all kinds of blessings on me, and I felt like a god.

When the first light of the day shone through the curtains, we were lying in bed, still awake and exhausted. I don't know if it was because of the fatigue I felt, or because of the implied threat in the latter verses of Hesiod's poem, where he talks about *the goddess withholding her favors sometimes*, rang true for me at the end of our lovemaking, but, somehow, all those emotions piled up in me—that hidden jealousy, the loneliness, poverty and my despair of it, all of it—suddenly surged to bring down the dam holding everything in check, merging in the process and taking the shape of a singular experience, that of my father's demise. I began to tell Hayat Hanım about Dad's last days.

"I sent my mother home at night and stayed with him. My father was in the ICU. We knew he wasn't going to make it, I suppose. Still, we hoped for a miracle. I used to sit on a bench that was just outside the doors of the ICU all night. When I got tired of sitting, I walked in the corridors. They would be deserted. Only after midnight, one could hear sounds in that gloomy place. The clacking of iron wheels. At first, I didn't know what it was. Then I ran into it at the end of a long hall. A scrawny man, blind in one eye, was pulling a hospital bed, with a woman wearing a headscarf in tow. I saw the silhouette of the human body under the sheet and realized they were transferring a dead person. They transported the dead from one place to another until dawn. The half-blind man in the front, the headscarfed woman in the back, they fetched the dead to an underground morgue. Whenever I heard the clacking, I tried to avoid them, but somehow they always turned a corner and found me there. Death on iron wheels kept chasing me, foretelling me with its mumbling that my father would also be taken underground in the same manner. One night…"

My voice trembled…I had buried my head in Hayat Hanım's chest. She held me tightly.

"Death doesn't scare the dead, dear boy," she said. "Like life, death also ends once you die…Only the living are afraid of death."

I was ashamed of my crying, but at the same time I felt lighter for it, somewhat cleansed and purer inside; sharing my personal sorrows with her made Hayat Hanım an inseparable part of me, I thought, and with that, an odd feeling took over me, undefinable yet extremely comforting. Relaxed, I could once again feel her body, her belly touching mine. I held her thigh. "What now, Antony," she said, and reached down with her hand.

"You horny rascal…"

That morning, I woke up happy.

"I have no classes today," I said at breakfast, "and no studio sessions in the evening."

"Well then," she said.

She had put on a thick morning gown and opened the windows. The fresh, cool air filled the apartment. She had shadows under her eyes, and the lines on her face looked deeper.

"No more staying up all night for me!" she said. "We'll be closed for business from 3 a.m., at the latest. Look at me, I went to bed as myself and got up as my mother. And you ask, *Why do you send me away?* Because you are going to kill me. That's why."

She carried on grumbling as she tucked into her breakfast. I could see her eyes sparkle with tiny bits of glitter, like diamond dust.

We didn't go out that day. The apartment was warm. It smelled of flowers. It was peaceful. We watched TV in the afternoon. A man was talking about how the Roman Empire became large and expansive. It wasn't because of its soldiers, it was thanks to the success of its engineers. They brought water to the cities from hundreds of miles away, transferring it over the mountains, plains, and rivers. She watched with curiosity, intrigued by the "inverted siphon technology" that had enabled the Romans' uphill water transfer.

"Look, they made the water run upward … How did they do it?"

"They were applying the laws of pressure. Whatever height the water drops from, it will go back up to the same level, thanks to pressure."

"Isn't that fascinating?"

She had an unquenchable curiosity, and with her amazing memory, she remembered every single thing she saw. Earth, nature, history—for her, everything was like a new toy given to a kid. It was as if the entire universe were created so that there would be an amusing tale to tell Hayat Hanım.

The narrator of the documentary said that Roman civilization grew and expanded through roads, aqueducts, cisterns, and baths. In some places in England, they still used today the roads built by the Romans. Their cisterns and aqueducts remained intact. Roman engineers invented methods to solve even the most complex sort of problems. Their soldiers marched on the roads their engineers had opened, crossed the bridges they had built.

"They never say the names of those engineers," she said, "aren't there any famous engineers in history?"

"It is the commanders who become famous, not the engineers."

"Who's the most famous commander?"

"Julius Caesar."

"The one with the red cape."

"Do you know how Julius Caesar defeated Pompey?"

"Who is Pompey?"

"Another commander... The two of them ruled Rome together."

"So why did they get into a fight?"

"Because each of them wanted to rule the empire on his own."

"Men's obsession with being greater than the other guy is so utterly stupid..."

"That is what history is all about."

"So how did Julius Caesar defeat the other guy?" she asked.

Once she heard something interesting, she hung on to it like a small sardine on a hook.

"Pompey had a great number of well-trained cavalrymen. Julius Caesar, on the other hand, had an infantry regiment equipped only with lances. He had noticed that Pompey's cavalrymen were all quite young. Normally, in a battle, lancers would stab the cavalrymen's legs or the horses they rode. Caesar, however, told his men to aim their lances at the faces of the cavalry. His soldiers obeyed. This attack baffled the young cavalrymen, and the thought of their faces receiving wounds and becoming unsightly made them disperse and withdraw. Pompey lost the battle."

"Was that really how they lost?"

"This is how Plutarch tells it."

"Aw, poor things... Had Pompey's men been old and ugly, would he have won the battle then?"

I liked talking with her. When we talked, the most serious problems of the human race turned into the laughable adventures of a bunch of clumsy fools. I felt myself a part of that idiocy, but at the same time, like a member of the council of gods who pitied those fools. She held a prism in her hands, and unknown to anyone else, that prism changed the shape of everything. Once she held it over something, whatever that might be, that thing liberated itself from a rigid matrix that had been in place for thousands of years and became part of an amusing game. Sometimes I really believed she had the power of a goddess.

But what business did a goddess have talking to a mob boss? I couldn't fathom that. Nor could I ask her about it.

7

My life had become a strange, uncanny balancing act. I was living alone in a boardinghouse room, yet there were two women in my life, even though my relationship with them didn't have a name or definition. What were they to me, what was I to them, I didn't know. We didn't utter a single word about our feelings. We neither made nor demanded promises. Each of them could give up on me at any time: they could easily slip out of my life.

Hayat Hanım and I went home together after each studio session and parted company each morning. We didn't talk about whether we would do the same thing after the next session. Sometimes Hayat Hanım didn't show up at the studio. She never said why she didn't. And I could never bring myself to ask. She let everything remain in limbo, and she did so almost purposefully, resisting the temptation to give a clear shape to life and the affair. There were no sharp contours in our relationship, nothing straight, nothing clear-cut. Everything could change shape at any moment, transform into something else or evanesce altogether. This kind of ambiguity was disturbing to me, but oddly enough, it was also a turn-on. I wanted to hold on to her and what we had together as tightly as I could. Alas, I failed to do so.

Sıla and I saw each other whenever she didn't have to go to class or to work. We walked around the city, and occasionally went to the movies. And sometimes, sitting in inexpensive coffeehouses, we talked for hours about literature. We were fond of the same books, the same characters, the same authors.

I felt deeply loyal to both Sıla and Hayat Hanım; and even though none of us had made any promises, I felt deeply guilty toward them. My inherent reticence helped me disguise what was really going on. At the same time, failure to tell the whole truth felt like a gross injustice. Inhibition had made me realize that keeping silent about things could also be a form of betrayal. And knowing they didn't tell me the whole truth either wasn't much of a consolation; on the contrary, it combined my sense of guilt with a good dose of bitter curiosity. I assumed what I was feeling was jealousy in disguise.

Both women were constantly on my mind, like two parallel lines of thought that never replaced one another. Yet those lines had shadows that did overlap. Those gray areas made my head murky, deprived it of its inner luminosity and dragged my mind into the twilight of indecision. Who was the source behind this mystifying haze, this mental eclipse? Was it I or them? I couldn't figure it out. But I knew, even then, that in the geometry of human emotions, two lines couldn't remain parallel forever. Sooner or later they would intersect. I had an obscure sense of premonition, the kind even total neophytes like me who are unable to unload their minds of shadows could have.

We didn't ever buy chocolates again, Sıla and I. She must have been more upset than she let on that day. We had become used to not having money relatively easily, but we both had a difficult time getting used to being poor. We were both raised in an environment where poverty was scorned, taken as equivalent to inadequacy and failure. Now that we found ourselves among the large crowd of pathetic nobodies, we realized how the wealthy people saw us. Although we didn't look down on the poor, we weren't quite ready to digest the fact that we were now part of the scorned, the destitute. Perhaps we would never be ready.

Hayat Hanım, on the other hand, scoffed at the rich. "Those fools..." she said with glee, "they waste their entire lives trying to make a fortune they wouldn't be able to spend in their lifetime." But Sıla and I couldn't manage remaining as unaffected and confident as Hayat Hanım was. We had grown up knowing instinctively that our fathers were rich and thus untouchable; that we would always be able to do whatever we wanted. Arrogance was our nature; it was etched under our skin with the first toy bought for us. No doubt the kind of hauteur whose traces I now and then saw on Sıla's face could also be detected on mine. We had not lost only our money, though, we had also lost our confidence in our lives. Alas, nothing could erase the hubris that had so deeply penetrated our psyche.

We avoided both the rich and the poor. We were particularly uncomfortable in the company of our old wealthy friends. This shared need to hide from them, in a place of our own, as well as our fondness of literature, must have brought us closer. We never mentioned these matters. We had quickly learned that one should accept certain facts tacitly, and that talking about them might make them even more unbearable. We talked about literature, philosophy, history, mythology... These subjects gave us shelter—the stories of the past were a good remedy for today's woes.

"In both mythology and religion," Sıla said once, "life begins with enormous violence. Think about it! Uranus impregnates the earth goddess to start a progeny of deities and is castrated by his son Kronos. Mythology kicks off with a son cutting off his father's balls! And Kronos is killed by his son Zeus. That is how the Greeks envisioned the beginning of life... Religion is no less violent in its portrayal of genesis. Adam and Eve are cast out of Eden. And before you know it, one of their sons kills the other one, because both of them burned with love for their own sister. Why do you think all great stories begin this way, with such utter violence?"

I enjoyed listening to her calm and authoritative voice.

"Because of fear, I guess," I replied. "Life must have been quite scary what with all those wild animals, natural disasters, hunger, and the cold... So they sought a savior, someone more terrifying, more violent and powerful than anything else they encountered. They envisioned a violence that would know no boundaries, something that with its enormity would scare off everything that used to scare them."

She pondered for a moment and then said: "Maybe. That makes sense, I guess."

She never accepted any argument before processing it thoroughly, so when she did agree with something I had said I felt rewarded. Her calmness and composure, her distance, her veiled arrogance, and her staidness gave her the kind of charisma I lacked. She fascinated me. She lacked Hayat Hanım's spontaneity; instead, she had an educated restraint, an attractive dose of sangfroid. Because her life had changed so suddenly, perhaps, and that she had seen how easily everything could change, she was always cautious. They could do more harm to her and her family any moment, she believed; *They will do everything*, she often said. She didn't say who *they* were. She probably didn't know.

One day near the end of November, we heard the sound of thunder as we were leaving a movie theater. The sky was on the brink of exploding with fury. The street was deserted; everyone had taken shelter somewhere. While we were standing on the sidewalk trying to decide what to do, the rain started, drops as hard as pebbles hitting us. At that very moment, a car stopped by us, the driver's window rolled down, and the man at the wheel said, "Get in, Sıla Hanım."

Sıla looked in the car and said, "Thank you, but we are not going far."

The man reached to open the back door: "I'll take you there, get in, don't get soaked."

"Come on, you too," Sıla said to me then. We got in the car and sat in the back seat, side by side.

"How are you, Yakup?" asked Sıla.

Then she turned to me and explained: "Yakup used to be my father's driver."

"Thank you, Sıla Hanım. Thank God, we're doing fine."

He looked about thirty-five, forty years old. Fair-skinned, slightly balding on the top of his head. We were looking at the back of his brown-and-red checkered jacket, made of some thick fabric. The shoulders were cut a bit too large for him, making the jacket droop slightly on the sides.

"Where do you work now?"

Yakup, as if he had been waiting for this question, leaned back firmly. "I don't work anywhere now. My brothers and I have started our own business."

He paused so Sıla could ask *What sort of business*, but when she didn't say anything, he carried on.

"We're contractors. You know, my older brother is the deputy chair of the district."

"I didn't know," said Sıla, coldly.

Yakup repeated himself with great pleasure. "Deputy chair of the district. And the mayor never disobliges my brother. So we receive municipal tenders and contracts."

"What do you know about being a contractor?"

"What is there to know in contracting, Sılacığım…"[5]

I felt Sıla's body stiffen. The turn from *Sıla Hanım* to *Sılacığım* had been rather sharp. Yakup didn't notice her reaction; he kept talking in the most self-assured manner.

---

[5] "My dear Sıla." "Cığım," a diminutive suffix in Turkish, implies informality.

"You hire the workers, put them under a foreman, and they pave the roads with asphalt."

"No wonder the roads always get filled with potholes," responded Sıla.

Yakup, pretending not to hear her, pointed at me with her head.

"Who's your pal?"

"What an odd question, Yakup!"

Yakup mumbled something in his mouth, something like *Just asking*...But it didn't take him long to regain his composure.

"How is Muammer Bey doing? I heard he works in the produce market now."

"He's fine."

"Greetings to Muammer Abi...Tell him he should let me know if he needs anything. The long arm of our family, you know, we'll help. My older brother..."

"...is the deputy chair of the district..." said Sıla with a tight grin.

"What are you doing now," he asked Sıla, "do you still go to school, or did you have to quit?"

"This is *us*," said Sıla. "We live here. Let's get out."

"Where do you live now?" asked Yakup curiously. "Let me drop you in front of your house."

"No need for that, thank you."

The car stopped, Yakup took out a business card from his pocket, I saw the word CONTRACTOR printed under his name.

"Sıla, give this to Muammer Abi, in case he needs anything…"

Sıla didn't respond. We got off and shut the door. Yakup lowered his head to look at us once more, then drove away.

Sıla's face was as white as a sheet. We leaned against the wall of an apartment block.

"Why did you tell him you lived here?"

"Didn't you hear him, his older brother is the deputy chief of the district," said Sıla in a nervous tone, not hiding her impatience with my naivete. "These people aren't to be trusted, they *will* go and tell on you."

"What can he tell on you," I said in bafflement. "There's *nothing* to tell…"

"Do you think there needs to be *something* to tell for them to rat on people?" she said. "You will get arrested the moment they rat on you. Then it will be up to you to prove your innocence… Where do you live, for God's sake? Look around yourself, will you?"

Rain was still pouring down and thunder roaring. We were standing there with our backs to the wall. Buildings around us didn't have a distinct color anymore, rain turned everything to a pale gray, things looked as if they would melt away with rain.

"What we need is terrific gods," said Sıla as if talking to herself. "Totally terrific gods!"

She sighed with resentment. "Have you got any money?" she asked.

"A little."

"I have a little on me too. Let's go someplace for a drink... The pubs on your street must be open. We don't need to have a full meal, a couple of mezes will do..."

We walked beneath the eaves. The street was quiet, since it was still early. Most pubs were empty, and we stopped in front of one of them. The place had a concrete patio with bare wood tables under a tin canopy. The rain had eased off a bit.

"Let's not go inside," said Sıla. "Ask them to put a table-cloth on one of these tables. Let's eat out here. I can't be in-doors now."

"Can you please set one of these tables with a tablecloth?" I asked the waiter who came out to invite us in, "We'll eat here." The man was visibly annoyed with the extra work our choice required him. "You'll be cold."

"We won't be cold," I said.

"Fine," said the waiter grudgingly.

He brought out a tablecloth and laid it down. I ordered two double shots of rakı, some cheese, cold bean stew, and sliced tomatoes. The waiter looked at us with a wry face, as if to say *All that work for just this?*

I added water to the rakı. We watched the liquor turn white. Sıla drank almost half the glass at once. We were lis-tening to raindrops falling on the tin roof. It was indeed chilly. The water coming off the sides of the canopy formed little puddles on the concrete.

"Do you live on this street?"

"In that building over there."

"Nice building..."

We drank up our rakı in silence. It was getting dark.

"What is your room like?

"It's not a bad room."

"Do you have a heater?"

"I do...I have one of those ornate old-style cast iron radiators."

There was a lull in our conversation.

"Let's go to your room," she said afterward. "I am curious to see where you live."

We went upstairs without seeing anyone. The room was warm and dim. Raindrops were coming down on the windows. When I reached to turn on the light, she said not to.

She took off her coat. Then her sweater. Then her shirt. Then her boots, her jeans... Then, her hands reaching back, her bra...

She was slender but had a well-shaped body. Straight, toned legs and arms. A flat and firm tummy. Small, perky breasts. Her nipples were very dark in the dim light.

She got into bed.

I, too, undressed quickly and got in.

She charged in an entirely unexpected manner, without any warning and almost violently. Her arms and legs were surprisingly strong. She was pushing me down and trying to get on top. She didn't say what she wanted, she made no sound whatsoever, and she enveloped me with her arms and legs. I was baffled. I let her do what she wanted. This was a very rough manner of lovemaking, something I wasn't at all used to. She was hurting me. Eventually, we managed to find a rhythm.

And only then, an unknown kind of pleasure, one mixed with pain, began burning inside me and soon took hold of my body. Her body was like a horsewhip. I found her vigor in bed and the slimness of her figure unusual and surprisingly attractive.

She didn't talk when we took a pause in between love-making. She lay with her eyes closed.

It had gotten dark. The rain was still coming down. We had left the bathroom light on and its door open. As we lay pausing, the light impinged on her taut, smooth skin, making her body shine against the room's dimness. She was gorgeous.

When we finally stopped, it had gotten quite late. She lay with her eyes closed. Then all at once she opened them and asked, laughing, *You're not hurting anywhere, are you?* She had clearly lived that scene many times before; it was her routine. She must ask guys the same question every time, I mused, and the thought made me somewhat angry.

"You are a woman, I should be asking that question."

She didn't respond.

I turned at once and pressed her down on the bed, tightly holding her wrists. She struggled, but there was no way she could overcome me.

"You're a woman," I said. "Now say *I'm a woman.*"

"Fazıl…Fazıl, are you crazy? Fazıl…"

"Say it, *I'm a woman.*"

"Fazıl, you're scaring me."

"Say it, *I'm a woman.*"

She giggled: "I'm a woman…Satisfied? In order to convince you that I *am* a woman, I need to say it aloud, is that it?"

I let her go.

"Lunatic...Look at my wrists...What's got into you?"

"I sensed something wasn't right in the distribution of roles, so I corrected it."

I was happy with what I had done, I was laughing, and she was too. "You're nuts," she kept saying.

"Got any cigarettes?"

"Do you smoke?" I asked.

"Sometimes I do...I'm craving one at the moment."

"I don't have cigarettes here, but I can find some easily."

"Don't bother," she said. "It's not that important."

I decided to keep a pack of smokes in the room from now on.

She went to the bathroom and came back. She, too, walked on tiptoe.

"Are those the farmers on their way to a dance?"

"Yes."

She kissed me, "They're on their way to a dance, we're on our way back from it," she said. That was her only comment on our lovemaking, and it was enough to make me happy.

"The one at the front looks exactly like a count," she said. "The one in the middle also has the air of nobility. The one at the back is a perfect punk...He seems the most seasoned among them...The one in the middle looks a little like you, but your eyebrows are thicker..."

She kept staring at the picture.

"And your lips are finer than his."

She was in a cheerful mood. Her emotions changed as rapidly as mine.

We lay there as though we were relaxing on the beach after a long swim in choppy waters, satisfied and exhausted, our hands touching each other. I felt her warmth passing from her fingers to mine.

"It took us quite a while to decide to become a couple," I said.

"Nope," she said. "What took quite a while wasn't the decision to become a couple, it was deciding whether we should do it in a boardinghouse room."

Her shrewdness was hurtful. It also somewhat offended me that she could say something like that only minutes after the first time we had made love. I couldn't say anything. Much later, during our third or fourth time together at the boardinghouse, as we lay side by side after having just made love, I reminded her of what she had said on that first day.

"Can desire be such a calculated thing?"

She was looking at the ceiling. "It has nothing to do with desiring or calculating," she said. "It has everything to do with being a woman. So you wouldn't get it. From an early age we're raised with the fear of defilement. We're given a long list of what defiles a woman, a list of indecent acts. Before I can make any decision in these matters, my subconscious would have already gone through that entire list in order to check whether or not my potential deed is included among the indecent acts. Is what I am about to do listed and cataloged appropriately? Has a judgment been formed on it? Overruling that judgment takes more effort than you can imagine. And I don't think this dilemma has anything to do with cultural differences; it certainly has nothing to do with being developed or underdeveloped. I bet girls all around the world have this subconscious list of defilement. And coming to a boardinghouse room is an item on that list."

She paused and giggled softly. "I must have desired you so very much in order to act incautiously enough to come here."

Her eyes were still fixed on the ceiling.

"I think I'm always getting everything wrong," I said.

She turned to me and touched my nose with the tip of her finger.

"And that, my friend, has everything to do with being a man." She laughed. "If you understood everything the right way, you would be too scared to make a move."

When we left the boardinghouse the rain had stopped and the street was getting crowded.

"Should I buy smokes?" I asked.

"No, thank you. I don't want them now, I just had a craving at the time."

I took the car and gave her a lift home.

She kissed me as she was getting out.

"I have class tomorrow," she said. "Call me the day after…"

She stepped out of the car, then she leaned in and looked at me before she closed the door. "And don't play around with others," she said with a laugh.

The next day I made it to class at the last minute.

Everyone listened intently to Kaan Bey as he talked, stroking his beard:

"Cioran has a very assertive proposition. *No true art without a strong dose of banality,* he writes. He takes his argument further by saying *The constant employment of the unaccustomed readily wearies us, nothing being more unendurable than the uniformity of the exceptional.* Adorno, on the other hand, defines art *as something that has escaped from reality and is nevertheless permeated with it,* adding that *art vibrates between seriousness and lightheartedness.* According to him, it is this tension that constitutes art. What's common to both of these arguments is the phenomenon that Cioran calls 'the quotidian' and what Adorno dubs as 'reality.' If we bring them together to make up the concept of 'quotidian reality,' we'll have what these two thinkers see as the essential characteristic of art."

He paused to let the class digest what he'd been telling them, took a few steps with his hands behind his back, and continued:

"The question that should be occupying our minds here is this: *What is quotidian reality from the viewpoint of literature?* When we say 'quotidian reality' we mean this very life, the life we all know and live. Can we then name the everyday truths of life from the viewpoint of literature?"

He stood close to the lectern and gazed at the class.

"Here are two basic and ordinary truths for you: clichés and coincidences."

He smiled.

"Let's assume that the cliché and the coincidence each relate to a single leg of the pair of compasses that we call life. When one leg is steadied on the cliché, the other leg, the adjustable one, will draw a circle made of coincidences, with all kinds of clichés at their center. The area inside that circle is reality—pure and quotidian. You can live your entire life moving about in that area *only*—that's what most people do…But if you just stay within those boundaries, you cannot create a work of art. How will you, then, avoid becoming hostage to the quotidian reality while you're being constantly permeated by it? How will you be able to create art? Please come to the next class meeting with your answers. We'll be discussing this all together."

I left the class thinking about the link between reality and authenticity. Was there an authentic reality? What could an authenticity that wasn't real contribute to literature? How could reality and authenticity coexist? My biggest dream was to lecture a roomful of students on such matters. What else could give me the bliss I felt when talking about and discussing literature? I remembered what Maxim Gorky said about Tolstoy—that Tolstoy didn't like talking about literature. *But the guy could write*, I thought, and he was never happy anyway. Talking about these things was perhaps the happiest thing about literature.

After I ate a sandwich at the cafeteria, I went to the library. Ever since I got the car I had been spending more time on campus. I didn't flee right after my classes. I studied at the library, thought about things and, read the books I liked. I liked the peacefulness of the library, the light of the green-shaded reading lamps on the tables, the smell of wood and paper. The solemnity that people here applied themselves to their work. Their quietness and concentration, the intensity of their focus, turned the place into a temple of worship for books. *There's a disciple in me*, I thought, *who has found his congregation in here.*

I checked out and read Adorno's *Notes to Literature*, taking my own notes from it. His views on Balzac and Zweig broke my heart, and I decided to talk about that with Sıla the first chance we got. My thoughts about her were now always accompanied with her naked image when she asked *Got any cigarettes?*

That night, there was a session at the TV studio, but I didn't know if Hayat Hanım would show up. She had not come the previous time.

I went back to the boardinghouse. I stopped by the kitchen to drink some tea before going to my room. Poet, Bodyguard, and one of the country boys were sitting at the table, talking. They stopped when they saw me. There are few things as hurtful and humiliating as people abruptly shutting up when you enter a room. I shook with fury, I felt I had been insulted without having done anything to deserve it. I turned back immediately to leave, but Poet called after me.

"Where are you going? Come, have some tea."

"I don't want to disturb you," I said.

"You're not disturbing anything, come, we're just chatting."

I poured myself some tea and sat with them. Poet had a staidness about him, a demeanor that was protective of everyone around him, along with a playfulness that spared no one in his banter.

"You're a student of literature, I hear…"

I didn't know where he had heard that, but somehow we all knew stuff about each other.

"That's right," I said. "And you're a poet, I hear."

"Me, a poet? Nope…Someone once thought that was a fitting name for me and it stuck. I kept telling people I wasn't a poet, but no one ever listened, so I gave in. I'm a copy editor at a magazine."

"A literary magazine?"

"A political magazine."

"Political?" I had not expected that.

"What's wrong?" he asked with a chuckle.

"Nothing," I said. "I'm surprised, is all. I had taken you for a poet."

"Well, you can keep thinking of me as a poet, but don't expect me to write any poems."

He got serious.

"We were talking about the situation," he said.

"What situation?"

"The situation in the country. Prices have skyrocketed, unemployment is high, there is no justice whatsoever."

I kept looking at him without a word.

"You have no interest in politics?" he asked.

"No," I said.

"But politics have an interest in you," he said with a chuckle. "You live in a boardinghouse, you're poor, they raid this house and arrest people. Why do you think all these things happen?"

"I don't know," I said.

I didn't know what to say.

He looked at our faces one by one.

"If you knew why all that's happening, perhaps it wouldn't be like this. If we had all known *why*, it wouldn't be like this."

"What can we do?" I asked.

He lit a cigarette. "We can begin by thinking about what we can do."

It was my turn to chuckle. "I'll begin thinking then, if you say that's the solution..."

"It could be the beginning of it."

"What happens afterward?"

"Perhaps you can help me read copy for the magazine in your spare time. They arrested the guy who used to help me."

He paused at once, regretting what he had said. He looked worried that he might have alarmed me.

"Do they arrest people for copyediting?"

"They arrest people for even less...I think I've scared you..."

I was scared, but I was also embarrassed about being scared.

"Nope," I said. "I'm not scared. I'll help you whenever I have time...But aren't *you* scared?"

"I'm scared. Of course I'm scared. But I'm used to being scared. I even enjoy it now."

It was hard to tell whether he was earnest or just pulling my leg. Bodyguard and the lad whose name I learned was Kenan didn't make a peep while we talked, but I sensed that Poet, for reasons unknown to me, trusted them.

I had finished my tea. He held my arm as I was getting up to go.

"The busboy," he said, "the one with the thin mustache? He lives on the ground floor, he gels his hair? Do you know who I'm talking about?"

"Yes."

"Be careful around him."

"Why?"

"He's mixed up in things. Not to be trusted."

"All right," I said.

I didn't quite get what *mixed up in things* meant, but I remembered Sıla talking about people who would rat on you: "Does one have to have done something worthy of telling to be ratted on?" All of that seemed unreal to me. I lived in the middle of those stories as though I was simply listening to a dull tale—a tale that hadn't had much of an effect on my emotions just yet.

That night, when I entered the studio, Hayat Hanım was dancing in her honey-colored dress. Her body was vibrating with such harmony that she immediately stood out in the crowd.

During the intermission, I went out to the corridor. I saw Hayat Hanım with a woman I'd seen many times in the audience. They were talking. They looked upset.

The intermission was longer than usual, so I bought some tea and sat on a plastic chair. Just then the woman next to me turned around.

"Why do you always sit at the back?" she asked. "You should sit in the front row—the camera shows those rows much more. And look at you, you're tall, you can find a job in a TV drama or something."

People surprised me. I wasn't sure what the connection between being tall and acting in a TV drama could be.

"Have you ever acted in a TV series?" I asked.

"Once they called me in for a wedding scene. I played one of the guests... I even shook hands with the lead actor."

I was at a loss for words, so I said, *How very nice.* When the bells announcing the end of the intermission rang, I went back into the hall. I wanted the session to end as soon as possible so I could be alone with Hayat Hanım. When I looked at her, Sıla's image flashed in my mind every now and then, but each time the image disappeared tacitly.

After the program, we went out together.

"Let's have dinner first," she said. "We can go home afterward."

We went to the restaurant with the sculptures. Cinderella, the dwarf, the giraffe, the angel—they were all there. Waiting for us. When we sat down I looked at her face. There she was, her ginger-gold hair and sardonic smile. I had missed her, I loved how the crow's-feet at the corners of her eyes deepened when she laughed. She was like a constantly singing muse. I couldn't grasp how she managed to always be happy.

Sometimes I thought of her as a naked little girl swimming in a lake filled with crocodiles, unaware of life's dangers, and I worried about her. Only a few hours ago, I had realized that I was also unaware of many things, that I was sort of ignorant about emotions, but I wasn't able to find bliss in my ignorance. What I found disturbing wasn't Hayat Hanım's ignorance, perhaps, but her happiness.

When our drinks were served, she raised her glass joyfully and said *absit omen.*

"Come again?"

"It is Latin. 'May the evil omen spare us.'"

She had said this as though she were casting a spell. She knew such unexpected things.

"Absit omen," I said.

I meant to ask her about that woman she had been talking to earlier, but something stopped me. Instead, I asked an altogether different question.

"What is the name of that diminutive clarinet player who keeps walking around among all of you on stage?"

"Hay."

"Hay is not a name."

She laughed, squinting her eyes. "His name is Hayrullah but that was too tall a name for him so I shortened it to fit his height. Everyone knows him as Hay now."

The mezes were delicious. She ate with appetite and kept saying "Come on, eat, this is delicious."

"How come you're always cheerful, always happy?" I asked.

She gave a small frown.

"What do you mean?"

"Life is filled with dangerous stuff and you're always cheerful, always happy."

"Does my being happy annoy you, Antony?"

I paused to think. Did her happiness annoy me? Did it make me angry? Was what I thought to be an uneasiness or concern in fact exasperation? To be honest, *yes*, she did make me angry at times. No one wanted the other person to be that optimistic, that happy, that unsusceptible. We all needed the other person to fret a little so that their anxiety would justify our worries and fears, granting us the right to tell ourselves that there was nothing despicable about *our* anxiety. Almost everyone around me had their own worries and fears about the future; I could sense this, and it established a sort of partnership among us all, it brought us together. But Hayat Hanım's sanguine detachment jeopardized that partnership; she would have nothing to do with the certain restlessness our minds had become so used to, and that left a void we didn't know how to fill. Not everyone could fill that void with optimism and nonchalance like Hayat Hanım could. She had no right to expect that from me. Yes, her sanguine detachment unnerved and at the same time embarrassed me to a certain extent...But it also made her attractive.

"What is going on, Antony?" she asked. "What made you get lost in your thoughts?"

"Yes," I said. "Your attitude does unnerve me a little, because you know nothing about the truths of life."

It was the first time I ever saw her get angry.

"Is that so?" she asked.

There was a long silence. She stopped eating. She began to talk rather slowly, as if explaining something to a stupid child.

"I know more about the truths of life than you can imagine. I know poverty, I know sorrow, I know despair. I know that I live on a planet where a delicate flower devours the bug that perches on its petals. I know that people inflict pain on each other, extort each other's rights, and murder one another. I know the truths of life. I eat from that poisonous honey as much as the next person. I swallow the poison quietly and savor the honey. Complain all you want, fear all you want, this honey is poisonous. But being scared or disgruntled doesn't make the poison disappear. It only prevents your ability to taste the honey. I know the truths of life; I ignore them, that's all. I swallow the poison without a grumble, and I don't mind the consequences of poisoning. Because I know everyone dies in the end…"

She stopped, then she smiled. "Come on, cut the nonsense talk and eat, Antony. Don't make Cleopatra angry. After all, I'm the one who let the snake into her bed."

"Am I the snake?"

"I don't know. That depends on what you are up to when I'm not around."

All of a sudden I felt someone grab my heart and squeeze it. I was terrified; I wondered in a panic if she knew about Sıla. Had she sensed something?

"Am *I* the snake?"

"What made you so worried, Antony?"

She looked at me intensely; a myriad of expressions I couldn't name moved across her face; she clearly had several thoughts at the same time—all unknown to me. She raised her glass and looked into my eyes.

"Absit omen," she said. "May evil spare us."

I felt like she said the words with a different emphasis this time. Then she spoke cheerfully, as though none of that conversation had just taken place. "Should we have sea bass?" she asked. "It's just the season for it. It will be tasty."

Afterward, we took a cab back to her place.

As soon as we walked in the door, that familiar smell...that familiar warmth...that familiar amber of the light. Each was a turn-on for me.

We didn't linger in the living room.

Hecate, the goddess with petal-soft feet, who bestows on men all kinds of happiness...

I put my arms around her before I went to sleep. "I taste the honey," I said. "Where's the poison?"

"The poison is in the honey."

The poison was in the honey. That was the cliché. Everything else was a coincidence.

8

I came out of my room after hearing noises. Two men were holding Gülsüm by the arms and dragging her. There was blood all over her face, her clothes were torn, her hair was a mess, there was a long run in her dark stockings, and her makeup was smudged around her eyes. "I didn't do anything to them," she said, sobbing. "I didn't do anything to them." She kept repeating that sentence.

All the doors on our floor opened, as everyone came out to the corridor.

"What happened?" asked Poet.

"The men with clubs gave her a beating," someone said.

Poet went to Gülsüm's side.

"What happened, Gülsüm?"

"I didn't do anything to them."

"I know. What happened?"

"They attacked me out of the blue. The other girls got away. The men caught up with me by the mosque. They beat me so bad, bro... They beat me so bad."

Apparently, she was caught because she wouldn't go into the mosque.

"Should we take you to a hospital?"

"No, don't even think about it … They'll beat me there too."

"Why would anyone beat you at the hospital?"

"Bro, you don't get it, they beat us everywhere. They beat us everywhere."

They took Gülsüm to her room and made her sit on her bed. Someone fetched a wet towel, then wiped her face with it, and another guy brought some cologne from his room and dressed her wound. There were many people in the room. I stood by the door, looking in. The clean scent of soap—betraying an extremely fastidious occupant, and floating above the acrid body odor of the single males standing around—reached my nostrils. I couldn't see the inside of the room all that well since there were so many people, but I could make out a small rug, in purple plush, at the foot of the bed, and under the dresser, a row of high-heeled patent leather shoes in yellow, green, pink, fuchsia, and red, all in size eleven. (They looked like scary birds that had bolted out of dark stormy skies. It was such an unusual image that even today the first thing that comes to my mind when I think of Gülsüm is her shoes.) She kept saying "I didn't do anything to them" and sobbing incessantly, as though on the verge of a nervous breakdown. *I didn't do anything to them.*

At that moment, Mogambo came in the room. Wherever he was returning from at that late hour of the night, he had his daily load of counterfeit handbags on his back. He asked in his African accent: "What happened here?"

"The men with clubs beat Gülsüm."

Mogambo split the crowd with his hefty body, walked over to Gülsüm, and looked at her. Gülsüm was pulling on the collar of her blouse and saying "I didn't do anything to them," clearly unaware that she was repeating the same sentence over and over. Mogambo put down the bags, gave everyone the once-over, and said: "You guys get out of here now, I'll talk to Gülsüm…"

Everyone else quietly left the room. I saw Mogambo sit beside Gülsüm before we closed the door. I went to my room. I could still hear Gülsüm's sobs. She calmed down a bit later… There was silence then. I left the room and ran downstairs.

Emir and Poet were in the kitchen, on their feet, talking. Tevhide was sitting on the table. When she saw me, she asked: "Who gave Gülsüm a beating?"

"I don't know," I said.

"Why did they beat her?"

"I don't know that either."

"Are they gonna beat us too?"

Emir jumped in.

"No, Tevhide sweetpea, no one will beat us."

"Let's go and have a drink," Poet said. "We can grab a bite too. And we can make sure to tell Tevhide that no one will beat us." The pubs were already empty. We went into one and sat down.

"Three rakıs for us," said Poet to the elderly waiter, "and a ginger ale for Tevhide Hanım. What's there to eat?"

As the waiter went through his list, Tevhide heard him say *lamb chops* and turned to her father excitedly.

"They have lamb chops?"

I saw Emir swallow quietly. The thin vein under his eye bulged.

"How much are the lamb chops?" He asked the waiter.

"Sixty-four liras."

There was a silence. Poet, smiling, looked at the waiter: "How many chops in one portion?"

"Three."

"Would it be all right, then, if you bring us a single chop and we pay one-third of the price?"

Tevhide was listening intently.

"I suppose," said the waiter.

"All right, then, you bring us a single chop. Also some feta cheese and sliced tomatoes."

When the waiter left, Tevhide looked at her father.

"*Will* he bring a lamb chop?"

"He will."

Tevhide smiled and said, "Good!" The waiter brought the rakıs and ginger ale. He also put down a plate of cheese and tomatoes. A little later, he came back with three lamb chops on a plate and put it in front of Tevhide.

"But we asked for a single chop only," said Emir hurriedly.

"The other two are on us," said the waiter.

Poet said, "Thank you" before Emir could react. When the waiter left he turned to Emir with a wry smile: "The solidarity of paupers! Wealthy gentlemen won't get it."

Holding the knife and fork with her tiny hands Tevhide had already begun cutting her lamb chop with utter seriousness. Emir frowned a little.

"You haven't offered the others any of it," he said. "You didn't ask if they wanted a piece."

Tevhide turned to us.

"Would you like a piece?"

"You eat it," said Poet. "We don't want any."

Tevhide looked at her father. "They don't want any," she said.

"They're being polite. You shouldn't be so ready to take their politeness at face value."

"What are you doing, Emir," I intervened. "She's only five."

"When is she going to learn if not *now*?"

"Don't worry," Poet said, "she will learn everything." Then he stroked Tevhide's head. "Go ahead, eat," he said. "Savor it." He raised his glass: "To paupers!"

He was only a few years older than the rest of us, but he had an air of maturity well beyond his years. Even when everyone in the boardinghouse was alarmed by something, he would keep his cool and reassure others. He looked like he was the sort of person in whom you could confide your most serious troubles only two minutes after meeting him. Judging by the loving respect the other boarders had for him, he must have helped each of them one way or another. I thought of him as a jigsaw piece whose loops and sockets fit in perfectly with the loops and sockets of life. Unlike me, he was truly a part of this life; he was intertwined with it, he knew that every problem had its solution. I envied him.

We stayed at the pub over an hour. Poet teased us about being *penniless aristocrats* all through dinner. He talked about *our class consciousness*, told us funny stories, made Tevhide laugh at his jokes. We all pitched in to pay the bill. We all felt tipsy, even though we had drunk very little. Tevhide was sleepy, and Emir carried her in his arms. As we were saying our good nights, Poet spoke with that wry smile on his face: "Good night, comrade aristocrats, we paupers salute you!"

The boardinghouse was quiet. It was dark. I went up to my room. I got up early in the morning. I didn't want to miss Nermin Hanım's class. It had already begun when I entered the hall. Nermin Hanım was lecturing while she paced the amphitheater.

"Criticism is an essential form of literature. You should never forget that criticism is indeed part of literature, and a critique should have as much literary merit as the work it criticizes, or at least enough literary merit to be worthy of that work."

She paused to look at the class.

"I don't know if any one of you will become a writer, but at least a couple of you will become critics. If there are any fools among you who think being a critic is easier than being a writer, I can tell that person right now that they have no business writing a critique. A good critic is harder to come by than a writer. Good critics are indeed a rare species. When you write a critique, you should aim to produce a work that can still be appreciated centuries later, like the writings of Boileau Sainte-Beuve or Belinski... You should have the kind of genius intuition Belinski demonstrated when upon reading *Poor Folk* he grasped that the book was a work of genius, and that it heralded future works like *The Brothers Karamazov*."

She giggled unexpectedly.

"But then, mere intuition is not enough to see the signs of genius in that early book. For that, one would need to possess the faculties of an oracle, which we cannot expect everyone to have."

She was serious again.

"You should also keep this in mind: criticism is not snobbery. It isn't a contest of understanding texts that no one else can. It isn't the profession of scorning the reader. In the twentieth century the critics glorified books that no one enjoyed reading, thereby turning literature into something that's beyond our grasp—insipid and boring...Borges taught *Finnegans Wake*, a book he was never able to finish reading...Do not teach anyone the books you cannot finish and do not write critiques of them! Good books have many known and unknown qualities, but the first of them is that they can be read from cover to cover. If you cannot read *Finnegans Wake* all the way to the end, that is a bad book for you...For someone who can read it, it might be a good book. What I call snobbery is praising a book that you cannot even read, trying to gain personal merit from the unreadability of the work you praise."

Hearing Nermin Hanım's voice and the things she said felt good. In other professors' classes I often got bored, but I left each lecture by Nermin Hanım or Kaan Bey with the same feeling: *This is the place where I belong, this school, these classes, these lectures, these discussions.* It was that sheltered world, which witnessed, knew, and understood life's truths, in all their ugliness and pain, and discussed them by adding to them a miraculous luster, a value. I could perhaps become the sort of critic Nermin Hanım had described, I thought. Although I wasn't like that in the outside world, here I was brave and honest. Nothing scared me in this place.

I met Sıla after class.

"How about fried mussels and beer by the sea?" she asked. "We can see a movie afterward."

The more she got accustomed to poverty the more generous she became.

I didn't know if it was because making love to me wasn't much of a thrill or that doing it in a boardinghouse still made her uneasy, but we didn't always go to my room when we met. Sıla decided when we'd go. There was no pattern to it. Sometimes we went two days in a row. Sometimes we didn't go for days.

We had discovered a cozy place by the sea where they made delicious deep-fried mussels. We went there. While we were drinking our beers I told her about Gülsüm, how she had been beaten and then kept sobbing afterward, saying repeatedly "I didn't do anything to them," and the way Mogambo made everyone else leave to sit alone with her.

"I couldn't have done what Mogambo did," I said.

"We all have things we aren't capable of," she said. "What's important is to know what these things are."

We never held hands, Sıla and I, never kissed or talked about our feelings when we were out together. I didn't know what sort of relationship we had. Nor did I care to give it a name. That vagueness agreed with me: it lightened the weight of guilt.

"The other day I ran into Yakup again as I was leaving the school."

"Are you serious?"

"He happened to be passing by. At least, that is what he said. I had to ride with him to the spot where you and I got off before so that he would believe that's where I lived. I had to take the bus home afterward. I ended up wasting so much time because of him."

"What did he talk about?" I asked.

"His ventures in contracting, how he makes a load of money... Remember the recent rainstorms? All the roads they had built collapsed... But he laughed and said, *There is a silver lining to everything.* The mayor awarded them the new tender for fixing the roads. He told me this proudly, without any sense of shame whatsoever... You know he didn't use to be brassy like this, he used to be an honest, reliable man. I can't figure out what made him change so radically. Or were people always like that and we just didn't notice it?"

Before I could respond, she asked me if I remembered Ömer Seyfettin's story "High Heels." I said *yes,* wondering what she would say next. She began to tell the story as though I had not answered her question.

"There is this wealthy lady. She is diminutive. She always walks around her mansion wearing high-heeled slippers. The sound of her heels can be heard all over the place. Her house is always in impeccable order, and the help are honest and trustworthy. Then one day she twists her ankle and has to switch to wearing soft, flat slippers. Soon after that, she busts the cook for stealing, and walks in on the gardener and the maid making out. The house is now in complete disarray. Only when she puts her noisy high-heeled slippers back on is order restored."

She smiled.

"Have we started seeing people as they are because we took off our high-heeled slippers?" she asked. "Was everything always like this?"

She paused a little before she added:

"Will everything be back in order if we could put our noisy slippers back on?"

"But," I said, "we also saw many good people once our high heels were off—people whom we hadn't noticed before."

She pondered this for a while. "You're right," she said. "Still, I'd rather be wearing my high-heeled slippers."

After the meal we went to the movies. We sat side by side in the dark, our arms touching each other. I loved feeling her warmth. After we left the movie theater, we bought coffee in paper cups, and she asked me what time it was. I looked at the clock on the wall in front of us and told her.

"It got late," she said. "Otherwise we could go to your place."

"That would have been nice," I said.

"What are your farmers doing?"

"They're going to a dance…"

She squeezed my arm gently.

"Next time we should go too."

This sense of closeness was absolutely the sweetest feeling. The intimacy between two people, the ability to say things that can't be said to anyone else or repeated in the presence of others, a naked display no one else would be allowed to see, never failed to arouse me. Women knew all too well how to create this emotion.

I saw Sıla to her home and went back to my building. I looked in the kitchen; Poet was just about to leave.

"I'll bring you a couple of articles for proofreading... Unless you have changed your mind, that is."

"Bring them," I said. "I haven't changed my mind."

I went up to my room. My farmers were there. They were the kind of people I could trust to always be there. There was a recording session at the studio that evening. I wondered if Hayat Hanım would come.

She didn't show up.

There was an odd vibe in the hall. The audience clapped and danced as usual, but everyone seemed clumsy somehow, as if something was bothering them. During the intermission, I went out to the corridor, and it was very quiet. People weren't talking. I went to the woman who thought I could be an actor on account of my height. "What's going on?" I asked. "Everyone seems so down." She gave a sigh.

"Kalender's daughter died."

"Who is Kalender?"

"You must have seen her. A quiet woman. Youngish. Calm. She usually sits on the right."

I remembered her. She was the woman I saw talking to Hayat Hanım a few days ago at the backstage door.

"Why did her daughter die?"

"She had measles."

"Who dies of measles in this day and age?"

"They gave her the wrong medicine," said the woman. "Poor child. Her funeral is tomorrow. We're all going."

"May I come too?"

"Of course, do come! Weddings and funerals... The more people attend them the better. The service will be after the noon prayers."

I took the address of the mosque from her.

A single incident can sometimes open a door in a person's mind. Through that door they can look inside and see all the cracks and depressions, all the quagmires of their soul in the clearest and most horrifying way. I was going to go to the funeral of an ill-fated child to see Hayat Hanım. Had I been sure she wouldn't go I wouldn't have gone either. Using a child's funeral to one's own benefit was despicable. It was as clear as day, there was no gray area that could give me refuge, no excuse to be made for my behavior. I had stumbled on my true self, and it put me in shame.

That night and throughout the following day, I considered not going to the funeral. Alas, then in the name of honesty, I would have missed the opportunity to join the others in consoling a grieving mother and that too would have been selfish. I was twisting myself into such bizarre contortions that coming out of them as righteous and decent was impossible.

I went to the funeral.

The mosque, near a cemetery on the outskirts of the city, was small, as compact as a stone in a ring, with slender minarets and an elegant fountain, manifesting both simplicity and eternity. A benefactor with good taste must have had it built so that the destitute could bid farewell to this world in a kind of elegance they may have never found in life. Hayat Hanım was there. Clad in black pants and a black blazer. Like all other women at the service, she had covered her head with a scarf. She was standing beside Kalender with one arm around her. Kalender looked exhausted. Once or twice she tottered in her place, and Hayat Hanım held her each time.

After they performed the funeral prayers, the men gathered to carry the coffin. I too held a corner. It was so light. Its lack of heft was so painful.

At the grave site Kalender suddenly broke down.

"Put me in the ground with my daughter," she screeched. "Where are you going, my girl? Where are you going, baby?"

I thought of Tolstoy, imagined him running across the prairie, shouting *There is no death, there is no death*, after his seven-year-old son died. They closed the grave. Kalender's relatives took her away. The small crowd dispersed among the graves like smoke.

Names were engraved on the tombstones, erected in the dark-green shadow of cypresses. Some stones had pictures of the persons lying there. Why did they gather all the dead and bury them in one place, I wondered. All these people were alive once. A tired cliché, stale enough to be ridiculous. On the other hand, it was by coincidence that they had all been gathered in this cemetery to lie side by side. They didn't know they would be buried in these graves side by side. They were destined to spend an eternity with thousands of people they had never known. They would be with these strangers for much longer than they had been with their loved ones. Their dead bodies would give life here to the same trees, the same bugs, the same flowers. For a moment, I had a mental image of all the dead rising from their graves. Thousands of them staring at each other in disbelief. Probably trying to cover their private parts. Vexed by their nakedness, rather than their demise. Unable to enjoy being dead. How did, I wondered, death become such a cliché that it no longer merited discussion? Everyone believed that they knew what death was, I supposed. No one thought it odd to believe that, when in fact they didn't know the first thing about it.

Hayat Hanım and I started walking among the tombstones. She had kept her scarf on.

"There is this great writer who, at the news of losing his child, went running in the prairie, shouting *There is no death, there is no death.*"

"There *is* death," she said.

Most graves were in good shape, with flowers adorning them. Hayat Hanım walked toward one with dry weeds over it. A woman's grave. She pulled the weeds. She took out some wet wipes from her purse and dusted off the tombstone. She called one of the boys with plastic pitchers, gave him some money to water the earth covering the grave. She took some flowers from the neighboring graves and put them on this one. She took a step back to have a look. I thought it was her mother's grave.

"Is this your mother?"

"No. No one I know."

"But…"

"This one looked orphaned among the others," she explained. "She must have no visitors. I didn't have the heart to leave her like that."

Suddenly, I couldn't hold myself and asked in a sardonic tone: "Does she see you?"

She spoke calmly: "Does someone have to see it for you to do a good deed?"

For a second I didn't know what to say.

"You stole other people's flowers," I said.

She answered in the flattest tone of voice: "Honesty is boring sometimes. It isn't always just either. One should carefully consider when to be honest."

After we had left the cemetery, she put her scarf in her purse.

"Now we must drink hard," she said. "Are you up for getting drunk, Antony?… This time we'll really booze up! We'll drink in a way that's befitting of the glory of death."

We found a restaurant close to the cemetery. As we waited for our drinks to be served I asked Hayat Hanım if she believed in God. I had noticed that she prayed in the mosque.

"At times I do," she said. "But not today… I think sometimes God has no idea what's going on."

When our drinks came she held up her glass and spoke as if to herself: "I wonder whether he leaves the shop to his apprentice once in a while and goes off on jaunts."

We drank hard indeed. We were drunk when we got home. We went directly to the bedroom. "We'll take life's revenge on death," she said as we were taking our clothes off. "But you'll need to work hard for that."

We took life's revenge on death.

Before falling asleep, I saw Hayat Hanım cry for the first time.

"Children, Antony," she said in a whisper. "Children."

The next morning, we woke up tired. At breakfast, the subject of death came up again.

"Spinoza says that each finite thing, insofar as it is in itself, strives to persevere in its own being."

She pondered as she deliciously sucked the juices out of an orange slice: "Tell that friend of yours that whoever created that finite thing couldn't care less about what it wants."

"He isn't my friend. He's a famous philosopher."

"So he's dead."

Sometimes she had such staggering comebacks that it would take me a while to grasp what she meant.

"What do you mean, *he's dead*?"

"Don't you only call the dead ones *philosophers*? Do you call the living ones philosophers too?"

She was talking about philosophers as though they were sea otters.

"We usually call the living ones theorists."

"Do they get promoted when they die?"

"I don't know," I said with a grin. "Spinoza is fantastic. He is a great philosopher."

"What exactly do they do, these philosophers of yours?"

"They try to come up with a system, one that is capable of making sense of the mystery of life."

"Have they been able to solve the mystery of life?"

"They're all trying to come up with an explanation."

"You mean they haven't figured it out…"

I bowed my head. "They haven't."

She laughed. "Neither have I! Will I also become a philosopher when I die?"

"I doubt it," I said.

"Say I go ahead and write a book with a single line, which reads *You fools, there's no mystery to life!* Would that make me a philosopher?"

"I don't think it works that way."

"Are you guys discriminating against me because I'm a woman?"

She was teasing me, as was her habit whenever we talked about these matters. She was all giggly, obviously having fun.

"You're wasting your time with all those books, Antony," she said. "No one knows about life more than I do."

"Let's not overestimate the powers of our ignorance," I said, laughing.

"Fine! You've read all those books. Tell me what life is then? What's its secret? Its reason?"

She continued before I could respond.

"All right, never mind, these are tough questions. Let me ask you an easy one: Why do cockroaches abruptly change the direction they're moving in?"

"I don't know."

"Indeed! No one knows."

Her laugh was delightful. It made me think I could keep talking about philosophy with her until the end of my life.

"I watched a documentary about quantum the other day," she said.

"Quantum?" I said in wonder.

"That thing about those tiny particles, the so-called subatomic…"

"I know what quantum is. So there's a documentary about quantum physics?"

"Sure… There's a documentary about everything."

Then she got serious. "But they conducted such a weird experiment…"

I was staring at her.

"They call it a double-slit experiment. You know the electrons in those atoms, right? When observed by a detector they behave like grains of sand, but as soon as the detector is turned off they start behaving like light waves. If you are looking at them they're grains of sand, when you are not looking, they're light… Some fakers, those electrons, huh?"

I'd never heard of such a thing. "Really?" I asked. She responded like a little child would, "I promise! I just watched it."

"Those tiny particles have no rules, no order whatsoever. If tiny ones behave like that, can you imagine what bigger ones might do?"

Then, out of the blue: "Should we go to the farmers' market? We have nothing left in the house, and it'll be fun to go. I love the farmers' market."

Our conversation had begun with death then moved to quantum mechanics and culminated at the farmers' market.

"Well, you're not much different from those electrons yourself," I quipped. "There's no knowing where you're coming from or where you're going to."

"You can stay at home. I can go and come back."

I didn't want to be away from her at that moment. I'd never been to a farmers' market before. We found the place teeming with people. Inside the row of wooden stalls, fruits and vegetables of all colors were displayed in appetizing heaps. The sellers praised their produce, shouting and screaming, while at the same time splashing the vegetables with water from tin cups they held in their hands. A cool, fresh smell rose from the displays. The awning over the stalls, stretched between wood stakes, made crackling sounds in the wind. Customers moving from one stall to the next in search of the cheapest and freshest produce bargained with sellers. The crowd affected me like liquor does. Intoxicating. I was dizzy with colors, smells, sounds, and bodies. I kept bumping into people and apologizing to them. Hayat Hanım walked without jostling anyone. She ate the fruit offered by the sellers and bargained as though it was a game she played. She made the stallholders plead with her—*Come on, lady, that is way too low*—only to end up purchasing everything at its original price and giving me all her loot. I neither knew how to carry the bags nor how to walk in a marketplace. I dropped the apples. Just as I knelt to collect them, off went the potatoes. Trying to put everything back into the bags, I butted against the market stalls. Hayat Hanım watched me undisturbed, all smiles.

"Don't you have any pity for me?" I asked.

"Nope," she said. "Here you are, Antony, uncovering the mystery of life."

No one had ever teased me before with such compassion. I was learning that love gained volume with the least-expected twinkles and chimes. I wondered why that had been the case, but I was beginning to realize that I had imagined romantic love as something heavier, deeper, somewhat woeful, even. Whereas the love I felt for Hayat Hanım, while extremely powerful and happy, made me feel light, as if I could begin floating in the air at any moment. With every smile, every jibe, every sign of the disdain she had for almost the entire human race, I became more attached to her and felt lighter for it. I would realize much later, wandering about like a blind man, how profound a dependency this jolly lightness had created as it settled unhindered in my soul, and how ghastly a burden its lack would impose.

When we came home she said, "I'll take a shower."

"I should take one too."

"*With* me?"

"Is that OK?"

"Come on in…"

Afterward, I helped her in the kitchen. We resembled a newlywed couple, I mused, going to the food market, taking showers, preparing meals together. The thought turned into a fantasy. I tried to envision us married. It was such a seductive image. Had she wanted to get married, I wouldn't have thought twice about it.

I didn't know how to prepare a meal. I had no idea what needed to be done and how. My clumsiness amused her.

"You've read all those books yet you learned neither the mystery of life nor how to cook. You haven't learned the two most important things."

After dinner we watched a documentary about flowers. The narrator was talking about the tools flowers used to attract bugs: scent, looks, and nectar.

"What does that remind you of?" asked Hayat Hanım.

"I don't know. What?"

"Oh, Antony, you're so dumb. He's talking about women, of course. Scent, looks, nectar…"

The so-called bee orchids were, in Hayat Hanım's words, the *sluttiest* of them all. The flower produced a scent that mimicked the scent of the female bee. Male bees were attracted to it, and the orchid pollen was transferred to their legs. In return, the scent of that pollen attracted female bees. Nature was in a constant state of reproduction, a glorious perpetual act of lovemaking… This seemed to be the only reason for nature's existence. Nature was a go-between, one that continuously liaised males with females. I got that, what I didn't get was the overall objective. What could be the reason for running this enormous brothel in such a remote nook of the universe?

The next day I left early to go to school. I was tired but extremely happy. I went to the boardinghouse to change my clothes, and first stopped by the kitchen for a cup of tea. As I walked in, a sudden, immediate sense of alarm, unlike anything I had experienced before, overtook me. I felt my brain shake in my skull.

Sıla was sitting at the end of the long kitchen table.

Her face was white like paper. Her eyes were red. Fatigue and sadness veiled her features like an iron mask. The first thought that occurred to me was that she had somehow found out I had spent the night with Hayat Hanım and had come to hold me to account.

"What is wrong?" I asked.

"They took away my father."

"Who did?"

"The police."

"When?"

"Before dawn."

"Where did they take him to?"

"I don't know...My mother called a lawyer we knew, and he said he would look into it, but I'm not sure that he will. From what I hear, they're arresting lawyers too. They're scared as well. I didn't know what to do. I came to find you. You weren't in your room so I waited here."

Poet appeared, sleepy-eyed.

"Where do the cops take the people they arrest?" I asked him.

"To the Police Department. Whom did they arrest?"

Reluctant to say anything, I turned to Sıla. "My father," she said.

"Go to the Police Department. They probably won't let you speak to your father, but they may give you some information."

"Where is the Police Department?"

He gave us the directions. We left right away. I had taken a shower that morning, but I still worried that she could smell Hayat Hanım on me. I knew it was ignoble of me to be concerned about that at that moment, but I couldn't help it.

When we got into the car Sıla asked with an icy voice: "Where were you?"

"I was at a friend's."

She only made a "hmmm" sound.

The Police Department was a large, fortresslike building. It had a vast concrete lot where police cars parked, and there was an iron railing around it. Two policemen holding machine guns kept guard at the main gate. We approached them. Sıla began to talk: "Excuse me?" She was going to ask about her father, but one of the policeman stopped her in mid-sentence, not bothering to listen to the rest. "I don't excuse you," he said. "Go away!" I could never have imagined a person treating a complete stranger in such a hostile, hateful manner. The animosity in his voice petrified me.

Sıla said, "My father," but was again unable to finish her sentence. "I told you to go away!" The policeman took a step toward Sıla, as if he might hit her. Sıla retreated and said, "If only..." but the policeman shouted, "Still blabbering? Go a-way!" I grabbed Sıla's arm and pulled her back. Then, stepping in between her and the policeman, I spoke hurriedly, without giving him a chance to interrupt. "When people are released, which gate do they come out from?" The policeman pointed to a little door at one side. "There," he said, and then added with the same unwavering antagonism, "*If* they're released, that is... Now, go away!"

"Come," I said to Sıla. I could see a row of coffeehouses across the street from the Police Department. "Let's go and wait there, and when your father comes out we'll see him."

Coffeehouses are normally only frequented by men, but these were packed with women. They were waiting for their fathers, brothers, and sons. We entered the quietest-looking place. Luckily, two women sitting at a table near the window got up just as we entered.

"Are you leaving?" I asked.

"Yes," said one of them, "we'll come back later."

We sat down at that table. The little door was straight across from us.

"Are you hungry?" I asked.

"I haven't eaten anything, but I don't feel hungry."

"Order us some tea," I said. "I'll get us something to eat."

There was a patisserie behind the row of coffeehouses, I bought sweet buns and almost force-fed Sıla with them.

We began to wait.

The dull silence in the coffeehouse was broken up now and then by the chinks and clatter of empty tea glasses the server carried in a metal tray. The women whispered among themselves while keeping their eyes fixed on the little door. They were desperate. Uneasy. Speaking very quietly, as though loud voices would bring bad omens on the people they were waiting for. A fear sharpened by fury, a state of perplexity that, given the unknowability of what the future held for them, vacillated between hope and the lack thereof, between anxiety and sorrow, marked their expression. They all seemed to have the same face.

The day passed, the night came.

"Do you have your father's picture with you?" I asked.

"Yes. Why do you ask?"

"Let me have a look at it."

"But why?"

"Show it to me," I said, my voice sounding nervous. She took out her wallet and showed me her father's photograph. A good-looking man, he had an air of smugness about him.

"All right," I said. "If he walks out of that door, I'll recognize him...You take the car now and go home. You're exhausted. Get some rest, then come back."

"You don't look very rested yourself."

I pretended not to hear her implication.

"We don't know how long we'll have to wait here," I said. "If we don't take turns to rest, we'll both fall asleep on these chairs and miss your father when he walks past us."

What I said was reasonable, and reason never failed to persuade Sıla.

"Fine," she said. "I'll be back in a couple of hours."

"Don't rush," I said. "Get some rest."

We waited there for exactly four days. We took turns to go and rest, to change our clothes and come back. I went to neither the university nor the studio. It worried me that Hayat Hanım might have been concerned about my absence, but luckily only one session had been scheduled during those four days, so I figured she couldn't be too anxious.

On the second day of us keeping watch, Sıla asked: "Who was the friend you were with that night?"

I lied to her with a swiftness that confounded me. "I was with a former roommate. There were also a few other guys from our class there."

She gave me a look as if she didn't know whether to trust or suspect me. She didn't say anything.

One night when I went to the boardinghouse to change my clothes, I bumped into Poet at the door and we went upstairs together.

"Any news?" he asked.

"Nope, we're waiting... Have they ever detained you?"

"A few times."

"How was it?"

"Pretty bad."

Then he added, with a woeful smile on his face: "Lately, I've become claustrophobic. In closed spaces I feel like I'm going to die."

"So, why don't you…"

"Why don't I quit my job at the magazine? Is that what you're asking?"

"Yes."

"Should I leave just like that, even though I know what they're doing to people?"

"But…"

"There's no but… That's the way it is. Once you've seen the truth you can't run away from it. That's why people don't ever want to see it."

On the third night, out of anguish and exasperation, we invented a game. One of us would say a sentence or describe a scene, and the other would try to guess which author wrote it.

"Friendship affords total certitude above all and that is what distinguishes it from love."

"Yourcenar."

"Not only our faults, but our most involuntary misfortunes, tend to corrupt our morals."

"Henry James."

"Like the Almighty, we also make everything in our own image, because we lack a more reliable model."

"I don't know, who?"

"Brodsky."

"It is seldom that you meet men whose souls, steeled in the impenetrable armor of resolution, are ready to fight a losing battle to the last."

"Who but Conrad would write such a thing?"

"On the male side, he is right; on the female, wrong."

"D. H. Lawrence."

"Potbellied mushrooms!"

Sıla burst into laughter, covering her mouth with her hand. Everyone in the coffeehouse turned around to look at us.

"You crack me up," she said. "How can you remember that! Gogol."

For four days and four nights in a row we sat at the same table, she and I, eating sweet buns when hungry, playing games at times, waiting in silence for hours, our eyes fixed at the little door across from us. Our agony, distress, helplessness, fragility, each like a wire, interweaved itself into a lace of steel and linked us to each other. I didn't console her: we had become too close for that. Sometimes she would have tears in her eyes and would reach to hold my hand. We were like siblings now, but also lovers.

"I'll never forget what you've done for me," she said once. I didn't say anything.

In the morning of the fourth day, Sıla jumped from her chair, screaming:

"Daddy!"

A man was standing outside the little door. She beamed across the street and almost got hit by a car. I could barely hold her back.

She gave her father a big hug: "How are you?"

Her father had an overgrown beard. A pale face, sunken eyes. His clothes were dirty.

"I'm fine, my girl, I'm fine."

"What happened?"

"They made me sign a paper declaring I won't sue them to take back my property."

"Let's go," said Sıla.

We got into the car. Sıla's father sat in the back, and she sat in the front, next to me.

"Fazıl stayed with me all four days that I waited for you here."

Her father looked at me. "Thank you," he said. "You also must have gone through a lot of trouble because of me."

I dropped them off outside their place. "Wait here for me," Sıla said, and I did. She came back half an hour later. "Take me to a windswept place," she said, and got in the car, "a place with crazy winds."

I took her to a hill overlooking the point where the waters of the strait flow into the sea. "Wait here" she said, and got out of the car. She turned her face to the sea.

A stiff northern gale was blowing. From inside the car I could hear it roar. She stood there, her body against the wind. At one point she extended her arms out to her sides. She stood like that for a long time, giving herself to the wind. She seemed to embrace it.

Then she came back to the car.

"I'm freezing. Take me to your place now and make me warm."

We went to the boardinghouse. The pack of smokes I had bought for her was waiting there by the three farmers.

9

The three dancers on the stage wore red bustiers embroidered in silver thread. Their bellies were exposed. Long chiffon skirts with slits from waist down opened with each movement, displaying their perfect legs all the way to their groins. In tune with both the solid rhythm of tom-toms and the smooth, frisky sound of the clarinet, they took small dancing steps while shaking their ample posteriors—a fervid vacillation that made their hips look like autonomous creatures. As they moved, shards of light bounced off the sequins adorning their costumes. Then, all at once, each woman reached under her skirt, pulled out the national flag, and continued the same immodest dance, now waving the flag in one hand. Thunderous applause broke in the hall. Belly dancers waving flags were such an unusual sight. It was hard to believe those women were real, their breasts, hips, bellies, flags all fluttering in perfect harmony.

During the intermission, I asked the blonde woman I had spoken with earlier: "What's with those flags?"

A man who had wet-looking, neatly combed long white hair interrupted: "The flag is sacred."

"That's not what I'm talking about," I said. "Where did those flags come from? What does the flag have to do with this dance?"

The man spoke with a grandiloquent voice, as if he were reciting the Holy Scripture. "Once the flag is out, one doesn't ask where it has come from," he said with an annoying know-it-allness.

I wanted to say *That flag came from a woman's twat*, but I saw the blonde's face. She had a dull look, almost devoid of expression, warning me with her eyes not to say too much. What alarmed me wasn't the man himself but the fact that fear had permeated a studio, a place four stories below the ground where half-naked women sang and danced. I didn't say another word. Wherever I went now I was confronted with a sense of fear. In the past, I never saw something I had to be afraid of. I didn't know how to either be afraid or act bravely. Never before did I need to know these things. Still, what agitated me more than fear itself was the sense of humiliation that came with it. I didn't know whom I was afraid of, or why, but all of this was humiliating to me.

That night, when we went home, I asked Hayat Hanım: "Why did those belly dancers bring out the flag? I never saw anything like that before."

"Rumor has it that those men with clubs will raid the studio. I guess that's why they did it."

"Would they really raid it?"

"I don't know... It's under Remzi's protection, I'm sure, but those men might not give a hoot."

I knew who Remzi was, but I couldn't hide the vengeful curiosity that her ease in saying his name had awakened in me. Suddenly, my mind went off track. I forgot about the women with flags and fell into the gutter of poisonous ideas that had been brewing in me for some time. Whenever my mind tumbled into that dark ditch I had an excruciating sense of vertigo and began to jerk and twitch uncontrollably, as though I were having an epileptic seizure. I could control neither my words nor my actions.

"Who's Remzi?" I asked.

"You saw him once in the corridor, remember?"

"Friend of yours?"

"Yes."

"Is he a close friend?"

I knew that was crossing the line. Hayat Hanım gave me a warning look.

"Yes," she said.

"I can't imagine you with him," I said.

"And there's no need for you to imagine any such thing."

A lurking envy suddenly charged and took off like a mad stallion, and with my foot caught in the stirrups, galloped, dragging me on the ground. I knew it was pathetic, but I couldn't rein in my jealousy.

"But...A woman like you shouldn't be with him..."

"Who should a woman like me be with, then? Someone like you, eh? Go and ask around if you will, find out if people would think it appropriate for a woman like me to be with someone like you."

She held my hand.

"There are no rules to this…"

I couldn't have imagined that a simple, ordinary sentence such as the one she said would hurt my soul as much as it did. I felt pain, but at the same time, an inexplicable sense of curiosity that made the pain even deeper was brewing in me, growing and pushing me over a line I shouldn't have crossed.

"Have there been others like that man?"

She spoke in a distant voice: "That's an odd question to ask."

"I'm sorry."

She must have felt for me at that moment.

"The past is perilous," she said. "You can't alter it, and because you can't alter it you are apt to become its enemy and try to wipe out someone's past. But to wipe out a person's past, you need to wipe out that person as well. To kill someone's past, you must kill the person."

Suddenly she gave me a smile, a complicated one betraying a mixture of facetiousness and desire.

"Do you want to kill me?"

"Sometimes, yes."

She gently leaned toward me.

"Kill me *sometimes* then," she said.

I looked at her plump, ivory-skinned neck and imagined my hands squeezing it. The thought aroused me. It had never occurred to me that the thought of killing someone could provoke sexual desire. My mind was off track again, now climbing up an untrodden trail to reach a new kind of pleasure, an eerie one, one completely unfamiliar to me. I realize today that one of the pegs I held on to while climbing that trail was an intense sense of resentment. Rage was always there, among the plethora of unnamable emotions Hayat Hanım fomented in me—and at that moment rage was turning into lust.

Being with her I had come to understand that all my emotions would mutate into desire at her touch. This was a miracle of her deity's sublime powers. She had taken over the reins simply by ignoring the rules. She was capable of effortlessly stirring all kinds of emotions into a dizzying vortex of desire. Whatever my initial reaction to something was, with her in the lead I always arrived at the same place.

Hayat Hanım was staring at me. It felt like she could actually see my every emotion on my face.

"Would you like to go to the bedroom?"

"Yes."

"Are you going to kill me?"

"Yes."

I killed her. That day and many times after that, I killed her. She looked straight into my eyes when I killed her; her pupils dilated and pulled me into their abyss. I was metamorphosing into some other person. Someone I didn't know, someone I had never met. A stranger. I was discovering the hidden land of pleasure, the kind of place I couldn't even have imagined to exist. I arrived there traveling through the dark, desolate valleys of the human soul. I could lose my bearings at any moment, I could remain in that dark basin forever, I could go on living my life as someone else. Inside me, there was a dark side that wanted to stay in this abyss, to consume itself with this angry passion, with this self-lacerating revelry. Even today, in a remote corner of my heart, I can feel the same desire—now a dehydrated tree, nearly dead, waiting for a downpour to revive it.

I got up. She lay in bed with her arms folded under her head, pleased with herself, looking at me like a shaman looking at a patient she had healed.

"*O lady…who allowed yourself, for my salvation, to leave your footprints there in Hell.*"

She let out a loud laugh.

"What was that?"

"From the book of a famous Italian poet," I said.

"Let me hear you say it again…"

"*O lady…who allowed yourself, for my salvation, to leave your footprints there in Hell.*"

"Am I to be offended or pleased by that?"

"As you wish," I said.

She got up and examined herself in the mirror.

"You left bruises on my neck, I'll have to wear a scarf…" she said. "Let's have coffee."

When I went back to the boardinghouse, Poet was sitting in the kitchen with someone. He invited me in: *There you are, we've been waiting for you.* I poured myself some tea and joined them at the table.

"This is Mümtaz," he said. "We work together at the magazine. I'm going to my hometown tomorrow, and I'll be gone for a while. Mümtaz will bring you the articles for proofreading... You haven't changed your mind, have you?"

"No."

"Good. You'll proof them, and Mümtaz will come and take them back from you."

"All right."

"Don't leave them lying around. The magazine is legit, there is nothing illegal about it, but it's better not to leave anything around."

"All right," I said again.

He smiled like a proud father. "Take care," he said, tapping me on the shoulder, "I'll see you when I'm back."

That is how we parted. At the time, none of us knew about the gruesome seed growing inside that perfectly tranquil night.

I woke up to people speaking loudly and shouting. It was dawn. I opened my door. The corridor was full of cops. Six of them were at Poet's door, pounding it and shouting: "Police! Open the door!"

Everyone else's doors were open. The only one that remained closed was Poet's. One of the cops shouted, "We'll break the door down if you don't open it." Not a sound from inside.

I closed my door and hurried to the balcony. Poet's room was three rooms away from mine. I could see his balcony.

First, I looked down. Police cars with flashing lights had filled up the street. Scary streaks of blue-and-red lights bounced off the walls and multiplied. Then I looked up toward

Poet's balcony. He was there in a flimsy shirt. The cops below had also spotted him. Speaking in their walkie-talkies, they informed their men inside the building: "On the balcony." I could also hear the cops inside kicking. Poet's door cracked.

He was standing on the balcony. I found his composure unnerving. As if he had come out to watch the sunrise on a summer morning. I was looking at him. I was concerned that the cops were outraged by his refusal to open his door and that they would make him pay for it. "Open your door!" I wanted to say to him, but no sound came out of my throat.

Our eyes met. I saw the blankness of his. He was looking but not seeing me. He was contemplating something.

Once I had asked him what his greatest dream was.

"To address a rally of millions of people," he said. "To tell them the truth from the dais and see in their faces that they grasp it, the truth."

It looked as if he were getting ready to give the speech of his dreams on that balcony. For a second, I believed that and waited for him to speak.

His room door was about to shatter.

He pressed against the wall with one hand and calmly climbed up on the railing. The police below were quiet now; they were watching him. He took a deep breath, looked at the sky, then turned toward me. His face was clear like glass. I saw the reflection of clouds on his face.

I stretched my hand out to him, but we were too far apart.

Suddenly, he pushed the wall he was leaning against and let himself go.

He landed a few feet away from the police cars. I heard him hit the ground. He squirmed one last time before his body went limp. One of his legs was bent, and his arms were spread out in both directions. Blood was gushing out of a cut on his temple.

I wanted to go inside at once, but I couldn't move. I looked at him. It felt to me that the sole manifestation of our friendship at that moment was me looking at his dead body. Looking was my act of defiance against those who had killed him.

I felt a profound sense of regret. As if I could have held him but had allowed him to slip away from between my hands. Had I screamed at that moment I could have stopped him, perhaps. Alas, my voice had not come out. My eyes had watched him slide into the void.

The police had broken down his door and were now on his balcony. They were looking down. I was looking at them. One of them noticed me.

"What are you looking at? Go inside."

I kept looking. He turned to the other cops and said, "Let's take that one," pointing at me. Another one said, "Let it go. We'll already have our hands full with all the reporting."

The cops left.

I remained on the balcony. I was shaking with a chill, and sadness and fear.

"Had he left a day earlier, he wouldn't have been caught," I thought, "even if he had left last night he would have survived." Why didn't he go away earlier? After a while, I realized that it would have made no difference. The police knew when he was going to leave. Had he attempted to leave yesterday they would have come yesterday; if he had decided to go tomorrow, they would have come tomorrow. They wanted to frustrate him, to break him, and perhaps even to make fun of him.

The sky was overcast. Sunbeams passing through the gaps in the clouds. The day was breaking. The street was deserted. Only a darkening trace of blood remained where Poet had hit the ground.

I left the room and rushed downstairs.

Everyone was in the kitchen. They were sitting around the table, possessed with the kind of disbelief, bewilderment, and horror one felt in the face of sudden death. Gülsüm wept quietly. The guys were telling versions of the same story to one another, over and over again, the way they each had lived it.

The busboy whom Poet had thought to be a *dubious person* spoke: "Why in the world did he jump? That was foolish of him, I think."

No one responded. I was going to say "He couldn't take being locked up," but I held back.

"Does anyone have a cell phone?" I asked. Bodyguard gave me his. It was too early to call. I sent Sıla a text message: "You awake?"

A few minutes later, she texted back: "Who's this?"

"It's me, Fazıl."

A second later the phone rang. She was speaking with a low voice in order not to wake up her parents, but I detected the anxious concern in her voice.

"How are you? What happened?"

"I'm OK," I said, "Nothing to worry about...Can I see you before school?"

"Pick me up in an hour...You're OK, right?"

"I'm OK," I said.

I needed to talk to someone who would be terrified at hearing my news, who would feel the horror of death and hate it. I didn't need to be consoled. I needed to share my horror and hatred. I picked Sıla up an hour later. As soon as she got in the car, she asked: "What happened?"

I told her everything. She kept saying—almost moaning— *Oh, my God, Oh, my God,* while she listened.

"If I'd shouted I might have stopped him, but my voice didn't come out."

"You probably couldn't have stopped him. From what you tell me, he seems to have made up his mind before he came out on the balcony."

"Maybe...But now for the rest of my life I'll think I might have been able to stop him if I could have shouted."

"That's not fair. You know that's not the case."

I bought her a sandwich from a patisserie. I didn't want any myself, but she made me eat half of it.

"Fazıl, we cannot go on living here like this," she said. "It gets worse every day. They're definitely not giving my parents' passports back, but I think I'll be able to get mine. Do you have a passport?"

"I do."

"Do you have visas?"

I smiled with sorrow.

"I do," I said. I'd gotten all the necessary visas in the days my father was wealthy.

"I'm corresponding with Hakan," she said. "I will apply to his college. You should apply there too. Your grades are good, they'll accept you. We can go together. We can work at jobs and go to school at the same time."

"I don't know," I said. "Let me think about it."

"Think about it, but think about it *seriously*... There's no future here."

"You know what," I said, "the image of him slipping off the balcony into the emptiness is constantly on my mind. As if he slipped from between my hands. I couldn't hold him."

She gave a sigh. "You couldn't have," she said. "No one could."

Then she asked with concern: "They won't do anything to you for being friends with him, will they?"

"They won't go that far," I said.

"They will do anything," she responded.

I didn't tell her I'd taken over Poet's job. If I'd mentioned that she would have been even more upset.

"If you'd like I can skip my class to stay with you," she said.

"That's OK. You go... We'll see each other tomorrow."

I dropped her off at her school. Her voice, rather than her words, had helped me calm down a little. But once she left my side the horror of death came back to haunt me.

Watching Poet jump off the railing, I, too, had become part of his death. I had skated along with him to the line where life ends and the quietus begins. Poet had crossed that line; I had stopped at it. Now I could neither move toward death nor go back to living. Something in me kept jumping and free-falling into that void, each time to stop just before hitting the ground and bounce back. I was living an incomplete death. Each time I bounced back, my incomplete death crashed into my life, demolishing certain things in me, changing them forever. Death was no longer a game, it was now a terrifying truth that had settled in me. It was in the depths of my being and it gave a new shape to everything else in there. I couldn't stop these free falls.

Once you get so close to death, time slows down. Ideas and emotions that you embraced as the only truth in your life no longer have their former weight and pace. The only thing that has remained unchanged in me is the guilt I felt for not being able to hold on to Poet.

That evening, I ran into Emir and Tevhide in front of the building.

"Come up with us," said Emir. "I'll put Tevhide down to sleep. We can talk afterward."

"OK," I said. We both needed to talk. Tevhide held my hand going upstairs.

"Poet died," she said. I looked at Emir.

"I told her," said Emir.

"Yes," I said. "He died."

"My mom also died," Tevhide said.

Then she paused and asked the question which must have been on her mind for a while: "Are we going to die too?"

"Someday."

"Which day?"

"I don't know."

"Why is everyone dying?"

"I don't know."

"Those who die go to the sky. My grandma said so!"

She seemed to be waiting for me to confirm it. I didn't say anything.

Their room was in the back of the building. It had no balcony but was larger than mine, with two beds, a coffee table like mine, an old leather chair, and a desk lamp giving off a soft light. There were books on the coffee table.

Emir tucked Tevhide in her bed and began to read *Alice in Wonderland* to her. He was reading in English. Now and then Tevhide asked questions, also in English. I sat in the leather chair, watching them. They seemed transported to a different land along with Alice.

Once Tevhide was asleep, Emir asked: "Would you like to have some cognac?"

"You have *cognac*?"

"I've got a bottle. I drink some once in a while."

He poured cognac into two tumblers, two fingers thick: "Sorry about the glasses."

He seemed genuinely embarrassed about serving cognac in tumblers. I couldn't help smiling.

He looked at Tevhide. "Her mother was British," he said.

Then we were quiet.

He didn't say anything else about that, and I didn't ask. I had noticed before that he didn't like talking about the past. From what I could gather from the odd personal sentence that would slip out of him in group conversations, he belonged to a wealthy old Ottoman family. They had come to a misfortune not dissimilar to what had happened to Sıla's father. His parents were abroad.

"Why did the police raid the place?"

"He was putting out a magazine."

"Did all this happen because he was putting out a magazine?"

I looked at Emir the way Sıla used to look at me, with some pity and some anger.

"They could easily take us away just for being acquainted with Poet, let alone putting out a magazine."

He suddenly looked perturbed.

"Are you serious?"

"I'm quite serious."

"But this is utterly absurd."

"Absurd, yet true."

He frowned and said as if talking to himself: "There's no one to take care of Tevhide if something happens to me."

I remembered the conversation I had had with Poet. As I spoke, I heard his wry and mellow voice in mine: "You've lost all your assets. You're living in a boardinghouse with your child. A man died before our very eyes just because he published a magazine...How can these absurdities still astound you?"

"I don't know... I'm trying to avoid getting used to such absurdity, I suppose... It feels to me like once I allow myself to get accustomed to all this nonsense then I would never be able to liberate myself from it."

"Resisting the idea doesn't liberate you either."

"That is what makes all this so scary."

When we polished off our cognacs and I was about to leave, he asked: "Do you think I should move out?"

"I don't know," I said.

10

Everything was already shifting, but after Poet's death it seemed as though the pace of change had increased. I felt like I was drifting in a river. Its waters flew faster and faster around me, surging as we were approaching the chute. Only six months ago, I had had an entirely different life and was a completely different person.

Like those desert snakes Hayat Hanım and I saw on TV, I, too, was shedding my skin. I was losing my past persona and my past emotions. I was still myself, but now with a new skin, with feelings that were more complicated than before. Old feelings remained buried in me somewhere; they were there but completely bereft of life. My only remaining connection to those feelings was that they once used to belong to me. When I thought about that bygone sense of safety and those feelings that used to exist within that safe place like harmless wildflowers, I was bewildered. The memory of that old emotional space left me in total disbelief—a space that had now been completely drained of life, lost its shape, and been taken over by new feelings that scarred me deeply and made my soul bleed. *Did I really use to feel that?* I kept wondering in awe.

I had become accustomed to resentment, fear, vengeance, jealousy, lust, cheating, and longing. I was making love with an older woman who was trying to kill her past; I was thinking about creating a different life with a woman my age in a foreign country; I was copyediting articles of a kind I had never read before, my hands all sweaty with fear; I was remembering the friend who let himself go into the void at dawn and those quiet women who kept looking desperately at a small door; I was feeling the urge to help complete strangers for reasons completely unknown to me. All my feelings left deep marks in my soul, but I had no idea where those marks eventually disappeared to. I had no idea where I was. I would know where I was headed to only when I arrived there...

The more profound my feelings were for both Hayat Hanım and Sıla the deeper they sank into an enigma. I missed both of those women, I was jealous of them, I desired them, but I couldn't name the one emotion that was the culmination of all those feelings. As my affection for them became more intense, so did the conundrum I found myself in. I hadn't had such powerful feelings before, but I had always been certain about my objective in life. I cared deeply now, but I had lost my way.

Mümtaz kept bringing me articles. They mentioned the thousands of people under arrest, the poor folks without employment—stories about torment and the tormented. It was as if I had lifted the lid off life and found an entirely disparate mode of existence in there, a life that resembled what people referred to as Hell. The starved were setting themselves on fire in the streets; jobless fathers were committing suicide with their families, sharing cyanide with their wives and children; women who had adapted themselves to their new life in the city were murdered everywhere, every day by men who were unable to adapt; unfed children were begging in the streets; young men and women were trying to get out of the country; people's houses were being raided every day at dawn; cops were arresting dissidents; businesses were going bankrupt; workers were sacked with no severance pay; and all of this was being kept under the cover of a terrifying silence. Daily papers, TV shows, newscasts did not talk about these things. People were free to set themselves on fire because they were starving, but it was forbidden to talk about these acts of suicide. I was beginning to see reality the way Poet used to see it. I didn't tell anyone about this, I didn't mention it to another soul, I just kept it inside me as my secret identity.

The trauma of death had begun to ease off, and my life had gone back to its usual routine. I had come to view the disorder as the order of things. I kept seeing both Hayat Hanım and Sıla, going to school, taking part in the studio programs, copyediting articles for the magazine.

One evening, during the intermission at the studio, I went out to the corridor and was standing by the door. Hayat Hanım was inside, still on the platform, giggling with Hay, the clarinet player. I watched her from a distance. People were drinking tea and chatting among themselves. All at once, we heard a roaring sound. It was getting closer and closer.

A large group of men came down the stairs, knocking down everything in their way like an avalanche or mudslide in the mountains. Some of them were carrying baseball bats. They yelled with a rage that seemed unlikely to subside. They swore. Women tried to run back to the greenroom behind the snack counter. I saw the neatly combed man who had said to me, *Once the flag comes out one doesn't ask where it came out from*, greet the men with open arms and a big smile on his face. But when one of them struck his forehead with a bat, the smile on his face froze and he tumbled on a plastic chair, his body covered in blood.

They were breaking everything they could, kicking men and women, dragging them on the floor by their hair. Those who fell to the floor screamed in pain and begged the men to stop hitting them. I watched the bats going up and down. I heard the sound of bones breaking. Blood poured freely, forming small puddles on the floor.

While I was looking around, frozen in awe, a fist landed on my cheekbone. I retreated slightly, and then with all the anger accumulated in me I punched the man who had hit me. I had never ever punched anyone before. The man slumped down at my feet. A group of thugs encircled me. They began hitting relentlessly. I was hitting back. I didn't feel the pain— it was as if I had lost all my senses. What remained in me was sheer rage and contempt.

At that moment, someone pulled me inside the hall and closed the doors behind me. It was Hayat Hanım. She had seen what was happening and come to my rescue. After she closed the doors leading to the corridor, she locked them and stood leaning her back against them. She held me with both hands. I was almost unconscious. I wanted to go back out; I didn't understand that I should be afraid. Because my fear had become too great for me to bear, it suddenly disappeared. She held me by the hair and brought my face closer to hers and began kissing me. The ruckus was still going on in the corridor, but there we were leaning against the door, making out.

I don't know how long it lasted. The racket eventually quieted down. The men had destroyed all of the chairs and the snack counter, and broken glass was everywhere. They had given a beating to whomever they could lay their hands on and left.

The evening's session was canceled. People dispersed in fear. The white-haired man was taken to the hospital. My cheekbone was swollen, and I had a bruise close to my eye. Hayat Hanım and I walked over to the restaurant with the sculptures. We drank down our first glasses of rakı without saying a word to each other.

"Did you really kiss me when those men were attacking?" I finally asked.

"That was the only thing I could think of doing to stop you."

I knew I would never be able to find anyone like her. I also knew life without her would be lacking in so many respects.

"You," I started to say, but couldn't continue. She looked at me and said, "Let's have another drink."

Savagery and rancor had seeped into the routine of things. We were trying to leave that outside our lives. She talked to me about the last documentary she had watched. It was about giant water bugs, she told me; they were bugs who caught fish and devoured frogs bigger than themselves. As for dragon-flies, they made a heart shape with their tiny bodies and legs when they mated, thus turning their act of copulation into the symbol of love.

Much later, when things had become even more diffi-cult, on a night when a snowstorm surprised us when we were prepared to welcome the spring, she said, "The days we could kiss away the dangers are now behind us," while she kept arguing that I should take Sıla and leave the country. At that moment, within the brilliant silence of snowflakes fly-ing over the entire city, the voice of a *boza*[6] seller was heard. It was like a call from centuries ago. She shouted, "The *boza* man is here," and jumped up with such joy that she didn't even think about covering her bare shoulders before she opened the window to call the man. As we drank the *boza*, which smelled like winter, I said, "How can you say such a thing? Don't you remember the dragonflies?" Then she said, "Ah, Antony, those bugs, they live for a very short time, you know," and as always changed the subject, "Would you like a bit more cinnamon on your *boza*?"

The next week something that would change our lives happened: Sıla got her passport. Almost every day since Poet's death she had been paying a visit to either the passport department or the court clerk, or the office of the lawyer who

---

[6] A tangy and very thick winter drink made from hulled millet that is tradi-tionally sold at night on the streets in Istanbul. (*Translator's note*)

was a relative. In the end, an aging policeman turned out to be helpful. He looked into Sıla's file and gave her passport back, along with a signed and stamped official document concerning the handover. "There was never a travel ban issued for you. One wonders why they took your passport away in the first place," he said.

To celebrate, we went to have deep-fried mussels and beer. She was in a great mood.

"Let's go to see the farmers," she said.

Lately we had been going to visit the farmers more often. Our roles had changed. Now it was I who knocked her around. Being rough in bed agreed with me more and more. Had things turned out differently, I might have never been aware of it, but it turned out I had developed a fondness for wild sex. I would hold Sıla's wrists and push her down on the bed. She would say, "I'm a woman." My childish reaction during our first time had now turned into a game that got both our juices flowing.

"Yakup came by the school," Sıla said after she lit a cigarette. "He happened to be in the neighborhood, that's what he said. He was so insistent on giving me a lift that I couldn't turn him down and ended up getting into his car. I had to ride with him until that spot where I had told him we lived. I got off there and walked home."

"The cops now know where you all live. You don't need to lie to him..."

"Still...If he tells them just for the sake of it, they might come knocking again. It is best that he doesn't know."

She took another puff, relishing the cigarette like a die-hard smoker.

"He had bought a bigger car, quite luxurious...And he hired a driver."

She laughed.

"Guess what the driver's name is."

I searched my mind for Sıla's father's name; "Muammer?" I said.

"You underestimate Yakup."

"What is it, then?"

"Yakup."

"His driver's name is *Yakup*?"

"Yes."

"You're lying," I said.

She frowned.

"Have you ever seen me lie about anything?"

"His driver's name is Yakup? Really?"

"I'm telling you. It *is* Yakup... 'Take a right, Yakup,' he says to his driver. And his driver says, 'Yes, sir, Yakup Bey.' It's like a sitcom."

"So what's he been talking about?"

"Their business is booming. His older brother became the county chairman, so now all of the neighboring districts give them contracts. He proudly told me that they built the same road five times over. 'Sılacığım'—that what he calls me now, *Sılacığım*, 'commercial sagacity is very important. If one has commercial sagacity making money is easy-peasy.' That's exactly what he said to me. He thinks this country has never been in better shape."

She put out her cigarette and became serious. "Fazıl," she said. I had come to know that whenever Sıla was getting ready to say something important to me, she always began with addressing me with my name: "Fazıl."

"I have my passport and everything, let's get away from this place … The likes of Yakup won't let us live here."

I let that pass unchallenged. She continued: "We can get a scholarship from Hakan's university. I heard there were larger rooms for couples in the dormitory. We can both work and go to school at the same time. Perhaps you can be a research assistant and join the academic staff. We can take your farmers and gods with us too."

"I don't know … What will my mom do?"

"Perhaps she'll come, too, after a while. And you never see your mom anyway. You can call her from there as often as you do now."

I was quiet, thinking. She looked at me:

"We don't have to live together just because we'll go together," she said. "If you'd like we can get separate rooms. Don't feel yourself under any obligation."

"Why are you saying this?"

"I don't know. You don't look too keen. Perhaps that is what's bothering you."

I held her wrists and pushed her down.

"*I'm talking bullshit*, say it."

"Fazıl…"

"*I'm talking bullshit,* say it."

"Fazıl…"

"*I'm talking bullshit,* say it."

"I'm talking bullshit."

"You really are talking bullshit. Where do you get these ideas from?"

"I don't know… You see the situation we're in, you see what's happening around us, but you're not willing to get away from it!"

"It's because I'm thinking about it… I'm thinking about money, I'm thinking about Mom, I'm thinking about college. I'm thinking about how we can manage everything."

"I'm done here," she said with a decisive voice, "I'm going to leave. You keep thinking about it. If you'd like to come along, we will go together. I can't take this place anymore, I can't go on being afraid all the time and worrying about what might happen to us. I am tired of being scared."

She looked offended. When we parted that day, she only said, "Think about it." And I said I would. She was right, of course, I was getting fed up with everything too. I would never have my wealthy life back, but I also missed a life where my hands wouldn't sweat with fear while proofing an article. The peaceful promise of a place where dawn would be dawn, and not the time for the police to raid people's homes, appealed to me as much as anyone, but I couldn't make a decision. I knew the day when I would have to reach a conclusion was fast approaching. But I wasn't able to decide. Not yet.

Once Hayat Hanım had said to me that she didn't make major decisions; "I only make minor decisions," she said. "Minor decisions make me happy." I had responded by saying that there would be a time for everyone to make major decisions. "Yes," she had said to that, "let's hope that day will never arrive for us."

After I had dropped off Sıla, I went back to my room. I stepped out onto the balcony. I watched the street. The familiar crowd had disappeared. The street was getting more deserted by each day. People were taking refuge in their homes. Restaurants were half-empty.

The next day I went to school. The cafeteria was packed. Nermin Hanım had come to have tea. She had the air of a queen paying a royal visit to her subjects. She did this sometimes. Getting the chance to talk with her outside the classroom gave us a sense of privilege. She wasn't a pretty woman, but she had panache, what with all that sassiness and the kind of self-esteem that on occasion came across as arrogance. She had no doubt about her ability to impress anyone with her wit, and that's what she did—impress all of us with her wit. She lectured us from another level, almost, from high above us, speaking in such a self-assured and effective manner that one could be made to believe that literature continued to exist so that Nermin Hanım could give lectures about it. I reckon all of her male students had fantasies about her. And she enjoyed provoking those fantasies from a safe distance.

When I walked in, everyone at the cafeteria was laughing at a joke I couldn't hear. Right then, a wave of excitement rippled through the crowd; someone had come in running and shouting "Cops are here." Nermin Hanım grimaced as if she had seen an ugly sight. She stood up; "Let's go have a look."

With Nermin Hanım in her red shoes ahead, all of us students went outside together. Two police buses had parked on the campus yard. The cops had disembarked. Students in other buildings had come out as well. We stood in rows behind Nermin Hanım. Addressing the policeman in the front with a radio in hand, she asked: "What's going on, officer?" This was clearly her first time ever talking to a cop.

"Who are you?" asked the police chief.

"I'm a professor of literature."

The man gave Nermin Hanım the once-over, his eyes resting on her red shoes for a moment too long.

"Professor, huh?"

"What's going on, officer?" Nermin Hanım repeated her question.

"We have information that a group of students hung a banner. We're here to arrest those students."

The crowd began to boo. The cops also stood in rows. We were facing each other like two rival armies. We were tapping our feet like a herd of bison pawing the ground before a charge.

"Is there a warrant authorizing you to be on the campus?"

The man shook his head. "We're in for a fight," he seemed to be thinking. "We don't need a warrant," he said. "We have information."

"You can't be here…"

"Madam professor, I'm doing my job! Don't stand in my way…Don't force me to take action against you too."

"If taking kids away is your job, then safeguarding them is mine…You can't be here."

The students and the cops were now pushing against each other, chest against shield. There were more of us than there were cops. Nermin Hanım's presence gave everyone courage. We could see that the police chief didn't want things to get out of control. Nermin Hanım's demeanor had daunted him. No one knew who anyone was anymore. The professor's self-confidence in speaking to the police might indicate that she was linked to some higher-ups. That cop couldn't imagine an ordinary academician having the guts to object to him otherwise.

He gave it one last shot.

"They opened a banner that had illegal expressions written on it. Don't protect the criminals."

"Who are you to decide who's a criminal? This is a university. We educate people here so that they can express their opinions freely."

"Madam Professor, you're making my job difficult here."

"And you are making *my* job difficult! Please leave the campus now so that the students can go back to their classes."

Eventually, the police chief told his men to get on their buses. As the cops left, the entire campus roared with jeers and boos, screams and cheers. When Nermin Hanım turned back to go inside, a reverent crowd parted in two in order to let her pass. Someone shouted *Ave Caesar* as she walked by them.

The words *Ave Caesar* rippled through rows of students, the whole crowd rumbling with that salutation. For some reason, the administrative staff had not come out. Nermin Hanım, all smiles, clearly pleased with herself, said, "Stop the antics already," before she entered one of the buildings. She was gone, but the students didn't break off the victory celebration. I was among them, also shouting and cheering, but at the same time I knew fully well that they would make Nermin Hanım pay for what she had done. I worried about her. The cops would be back.

The others were less conscious about what had been going on. I was reading the magazine, that's how I knew more. The magazine had a section called "Proceedings" in which they published minutes of court proceedings.

A defense attorney had been arrested after trying to prove his client right in court. A businessman had been under arrest for nine months, but they were telling neither him nor his attorneys why he had been detained. They only thing said was "It's confidential." A writer was given a life sentence for "creating an abstract threat" by writing op-eds.

People had watched all these things play out without any reaction.

Auden, whom we read in our Modern British Poetry class, had written:

> the expensive delicate ship that must have seen
> Something amazing, a boy falling out of the sky,
> Had somewhere to get to and sailed calmly on.

They looked at the boy falling out of the sky and went back to their seas to sail calmly on.

I had also seen the falling boy, yet I wasn't able anymore to go back to sailing calmly in the sea. The image of the falling boy didn't leave me alone, it had settled in me, it had become a part of my existence.

What I experienced, what I saw, what I learned, all of it became so heavy a burden at times that I felt like an old man, completely exhausted. Neither did I understand what those people were doing, nor the silence of society. I didn't quite get what was going on. This gave me such a sense of fatigue that I often thought I was sick. When I felt like that I would go to the library and read novels. Reading changed the light of the universe for me. People and incidents became pure and clear, I could look at the world without being seen by anyone, I could touch the people in the novels without anyone touching me. I felt safe and strong, and that feeling healed me. Life seemed temporary then and therefore artificial. Novels, on the other hand, were genuine, and they weren't going anywhere. Each book I read changed the era and the land I lived in, and even more significantly, it changed who I was. I was able to rid myself of that oppressive feeling of being captive and reach unhindered freedom.

Alas, this sense of freedom didn't last. As soon as I finished a novel, I found myself back in this closed, artificial world, living among people I couldn't understand. I was one of them—I couldn't understand myself. I couldn't describe my feelings, I couldn't grasp my thoughts, for I had discovered that my thoughts didn't exist all by themselves, in a singular form; each idea was accompanied by another, dissimilar "real idea." When I thought of something, I was in fact thinking of something else, I was deluding myself. Sometimes I cheated on myself too, and I didn't want to face up to that: I preferred to fail to understand myself in the same way that I failed to understand others. Understanding other people was safer than understanding oneself, but that too was something I failed at, save for the characters in books.

I don't remember how we had ended up talking about this, but once I told Hayat Hanım I couldn't understand people, that my mind wasn't wired for it.

She gave me that sardonic smile of hers. "Atoms never touch one another," she said.

She used to do this on purpose. She would begin talking with such an obscure phrase just to tease me for my "ignorance." It amused me as much as it amused her. I knew she was about to tell me something I had never heard before and then link her story to something entirely unexpected.

"Nothing can ever touch another thing, I saw this in a documentary the other day... Even those things we think are touching one another remain apart in fact by an unfathomable distance, like a billionth of something. If two atoms actually touched, they would fuse and explode, that's what they said..."

She looked at my face and knew what I was thinking.

"Even at that moment we can't entirely touch each other," she said. "Even when you're fucking me, there is a distance between us. And I used to wonder why we didn't make the world explode when we made love. Now I know it's because we were not really touching each other."

"Is that so?"

"That we don't explode..."

"That no one touches another person..."

She became serious.

"That's true...Nothing touches another thing on earth. No one touches another person."

"I've never heard that before."

"Me neither. It was the first time I had heard such a thing...How can a person understand another person in a place where no two people can touch? So don't worry, you aren't the only one who fails at this, nobody understands anybody."

"But writers do. They understand. They make us understand..."

"Oh, come on, what do they understand? You write something then and make us all understand. Who would object to you? No one knows the truth anyway."

"But literature heals me."

"That might be because you aren't sick in the first place."

"But I want to understand you."

"There's nothing to understand. What you see is what you get."

"What about the parts I haven't seen."

"Curb your curiosity. There isn't anything to understand in those parts either."

And with that, she stopped and changed the subject. She didn't like talking back and forth.

Sıla was exactly the opposite. She loved getting into long arguments about all kinds of things; she took pleasure in that. One of those days, she did something she had never done before. "Would you like me to spend the night at your place?" she asked me.

I was taken aback. "At *my* place?"

"Yes. If it's not too much trouble. Otherwise, forget it."

"Why would it be any trouble? Of course! I'd like that. What would your parents say?"

"I can tell them I'm sleeping over at a friend's house."

After calling her mother on the phone, she told me it would be all right. I stopped at the store and bought cheese triangles, potato chips, two cans of beer, and a chocolate bar. It was drizzling. It was chilly outside, making one long for a warm place. And my room was warm. Raindrops slowly glided down the glass panes on the balcony door. We didn't turn on the lamp. We left the light on in the bathroom with its door ajar. We put our dinner on the coffee table. Sıla took off her shoes and pants, then sat on the bed, keeping her shirt and sweater on. There was something intimate and peculiarly seductive in that half-dressed look. On the one hand, she didn't seem ready for making love, yet we could also start making love at any moment. It was as if we weren't in a boardinghouse where we had to rush things, but in our own home, and we had all the time we needed. Her sitting there like that stirred up my feelings. I was aroused. That was her way of giving me a taste of what living together would be like, I suppose. Perhaps she wanted both of us to have a taste of that.

While we were eating our meal, the rain started to come down harder. The sound of raindrops tapping the windows when I was alone in the room was different from the sound they made when Sıla was here. It was a pitter-patter now, friendly, peaceful. This rain would make a person happy.

Sıla was looking at the windows. "I watched Ingmar Bergman's *Autumn Sonata* on TV the other day," she said. "I had not seen it before."

I had seen that film a long time ago. There was this phrase I recalled, *a butterfly kept fluttering against a windowpane*, which had impressed me for some reason. Whereas what stuck in Sıla's head was the remark the mother, a well-known pianist, made about a prelude by Chopin. *This piece has to be played almost ugly*, the woman said in the film. We began arguing about whether certain parts in a novel should also be written *ugly*. We had finished our meal. I took off my shoes and sat beside Sıla on the bed. We leaned against the wall, her leg touching mine.

She argued that every part of a novel should be written in the best way possible, because that was the way to make the narrative the most effective. I, on the other hand, believed a clunky part sometimes could increase the effect.

"A writer cannot write badly on purpose, it's impossible."

"One can do that instinctively…A writer's intuition can lead him to writing in a style that's slightly *off*."

We kept at it like two students arguing for rival teams in a debate club. It didn't bother us; on the contrary, we had a lot of fun doing what we were doing. Our love for literature had brought us together, and our literary disagreements enforced that sense of togetherness—we both knew it.

"Why don't you take off your clothes?" she asked. "Aren't you uncomfortable like that?"

I took off my pants and socks. Our bare feet were there, side by side like four little puppets. She put one foot against mine.

"Take Dostoevsky, for example," she said.

We agreed that Dostoevsky wrote his magnificent novels rather badly. Sıla thought his novels would have made even more of an impact had he written them better. I told her that his *ugly* narration emphasized the complexity of the human soul. She took off her sweater. The top of her breasts was showing through her shirt. We took turns laying out contrasting arguments and made out in between. The pesky rain had turned to a heavy downpour, its loud sound in our ears fading out only when we kissed.

We made love calmly that night, very happily, not hurting each other, not repeating any of our habitual moves, with no fuss whatsoever. We weren't in a rush, we were home. Everything was in sweet harmony. When we stopped, Sıla peeled off the wrapping on the chocolate bar and began to eat it. *Lavender fields*, I mused to myself. On some mornings, my father and I used to go horseback riding in the early hours. He was the one who taught me how to ride. *Put your feet in the stirrups, push your heels down, press on the beast's body with your knees, keep your back straight.* We would pass through lavender fields, lavenders now leaning to one side with the wind, now straightening up again, a landscape rippling in harmony. The fact is my father never liked farming. What he liked was reading history books. And horseback riding. "Why do you keep this job?" I asked him once. "Tradition, son," he replied. "Tradition is what makes and breaks us." With the typical impetuosity of people who dislike their jobs, and ignoring my mother's admonitions, he had invested all his fortune in a single crop. Then he died. Death was simpler than life, yet even harder to grasp. My father looked sublime on his horse in the lavender winds. He didn't look like someone who would die. No one ever looked like they would die. Once Hayat Hanım and I watched a black-and-white documentary about old movie stars who were all dead by then. They all looked so happy. "They're laughing," I had remarked inadvertently. "Because they don't know they're dead," Hayat Hanım had quipped back. No one ever touched another person. They buried the dead together. Death was a cliché. The mating of dragonflies had turned into the symbol of love. Copulation turning into love was a cliché. My learning this from Hayat Hanım was a coincidence. Hayat Hanım didn't only play games with life, she played games with death too.

"What are you thinking about?" asked Sıla.

"Nothing," I said.

"Should one make love badly sometimes, I wonder?"

"I don't know. Was it *bad*?"

"No, it was beautiful. I'm just saying."

It was still pouring outside. We started making love again, and the sound of the rain faded away. Fatigued but peaceful, we fell asleep shortly before dawn. Just as I was about to slide deeper into sleep, I was woken up by her hand moving on my groin.

"Are you sleeping?" she asked.

"No."

"Can you fuck me at all hours of the day?"

"Yes." I turned toward her.

The day was breaking.

"It's almost light outside," she said. "Let's not sleep now. Let's go and have breakfast by the sea."

The morning came in a damp and opaque gray. The streets were empty. We bought warm böreks from a bakery that had just opened, then found ourselves a café at the seaside. A waiter looking not quite awake yet brought us tea. We began to eat our böreks, making crunching sounds with each bite.

We were sitting across from each other. Fatigue left shadows under her eyes. Her face looked thinner; she was gorgeous. As if I were seeing her face for the first time I was staring at it, its incredible beauty, in disbelief.

"Are you happy?" she asked.

"Yes," I said.

"When will you apply to the school?"

"I'll do it today as soon as I drop you off."

She smiled.

"Good."

She stroked my hand. When she touched me I saw the lavender fields in my mind.

I dropped her off at her house.

Lies were a cliché. My telling lies was a coincidence. It was yet another cliché that every lie had its cost. My premonition that I might soon have to pay for my lies was a coincidence.

God could well be playing some songs in an ugly way, and that improved their effect.

I was exhausted. I went back to my room and slept. That evening there was a recording session at the TV studio.

II

She resembled only herself, she wasn't like anyone else. I couldn't possibly know what she might do next. I had long suspected that sooner or later this day would come, but all the same, I was caught unprepared. I failed to foresee what was imminent; there was no way for me to know. She had prepared a wonderful meal. The dinner table looked marvelous, it was like a detail from a painting of the Last Supper. The amber light spread throughout the living room, and fresh-cut mimosas were in a couple of vases. Her ginger-gold hair shimmered. "We should have been wild horses, you and I, roaming the plains in Poland," she said while we ate. "Over there, a young stallion and an old mare lead the herds together. We would have been happy in those plains…"

After dinner, she put on a short, smoke-colored nightie and did something she had never done before: she danced for me, her breasts, her belly, her groin, her thighs visible through the thin fabric as she moved. Each time I attempted to get up, she pushed me back to my seat, gently, smiling.

It was a long night. Singular. With a spell the recipe of which was known only to her she lifted the tulle curtain covering the world's truths, over everything I knew, touched, saw, and sensed, and delivered us to the land of a separate reality.

In the morning, an elegant breakfast spread was waiting for me.

At the table, as soon as I reached with my fork to take a slice of cheese, she began to talk without looking at me:

"I saw you with that girl."

For a second, I didn't understand what she had said. Nonetheless, I knew whatever it was that she had said would be life-altering.

"What girl?" I asked.

"The girl who was sitting with you at the studio. I saw you with her…"

"Where did you see us?"

"You passed by me in the car."

I had passed by her with another woman by my side in *her* car. At first, I was embarrassed, not yet terrified. I was ashamed of my selfishness, bashful for my sordid attitude, one that allowed me to see something only when someone hit me in the face with it. But my fear of the consequences of cheating on Hayat Hanım soon drowned my sense of guilt.

"Ah, yes," I said. "Sıla."

"Her name is *Sıla*?"

"Yes."

"Do you see each other often?"

"Occasionally… She also studies literature."

"You must have a lot in common."

Not knowing what to say, how to react, I squirmed like an animal whose anklebone had just been broken. "She wants to go away," I said in an effort to clarify that what I had with Sıla wasn't a steady relationship. "She'll go to Canada soon."

She spoke with the atonal voice I'd already heard from her once before: "Didn't she ask you to go with her?"

"She didn't ask me. No! Not in so many words. Although she did say this was a place with no prospect and asked why I was staying here. It wasn't all that serious a conversation."

She paused to think for a moment, then carried on in the same flat voice: "Indeed, she's right! There is no future here for young people. Are you thinking about going away?"

"I don't know. It's not that simple. There's the university. Then, there's the money issue. How could I possibly go?"

"Financial stuff can be sorted out. There's always a solution. I think you *should* go with that girl. Abroad, you can make a much better life for yourselves."

She didn't rant, didn't accuse me of anything. She did the most dreadful thing she was capable of doing, withdrawing herself from me as if there was no intimacy between us. She left me outside her life. She did this with composure, a calmness that was much more hurtful than any other manifestation of anger could ever be.

"I don't know," I said.

"I think you do."

At that moment her voice cracked ever so slightly, and I heard for the first time what sounded like resentment. We left it there. I put on my clothes. As I was leaving I put the car keys on the table. She saw me doing it, but didn't say a word.

Outside her door, I felt completely alone. I also felt a peculiar sense of indignation, as if I wasn't the cheater, as if someone had betrayed me, leaving me at a moment I least expected. I wanted to go back in, but I knew she would greet me with that paralyzing grin. I wouldn't be able to cut through that shield to reach her. I had lost her.

Realizing all of a sudden that I in fact knew nothing about her made my sense of loneliness worse. I didn't know where she was born, who her family was, what she had lived through, whether she had any relatives. She hadn't answered any of my personal questions: she had brushed off all my queries by saying *There's nothing interesting in my life* and made fun of my curiosity.

I had asked her once if she had ever been married.

"Two or three times," she said, laughing.

"One doesn't get married two or three times," I said. "One may get married twice. One may get married three times. But not two *or* three times."

"OK. Let's say three times."

I didn't know if she had ever been married. Not even that. Once when we were buying meat she told the butcher that her own father was a butcher too. Later, she baffled me by telling a florist that her father was also a florist.

"You said your father was a butcher."

"When did I say that?"

"When we were buying meat."

"Oh, well. I must have lied," she said, shrugging her shoulders. It was as if her past didn't matter at all. She treated the past like Play-Doh, amusing herself by making different shapes from it. Because she had no interest in her own personal history, she believed no one else should be interested in it. The only clue I had about her past life was that man I saw at the studio. A piece of information that was good for nothing except for increasing my sense of isolation. Why in the world had she been with a man like that? Would she be with someone like that again after me? Would she listen to his crass talk and laugh at his crass jokes? Would he treat her badly? I wanted to protect her from such men, although I knew that if I had told her so, she would have had a good laugh. "I can protect myself, Antony," she would say. "You take care of Rome."

I thought I would never see Hayat Hanım again. I'd become sure of that when she didn't show up at the studio two nights in a row. I didn't know what to do. "Did you know that there's a black hole located at the center of each galaxy?" she had said to me once. "Galaxies form and evolve around those black holes and eventually disappear into them." Then, with her voice picking up that erudite tone, which surprised me every time I heard it, she said: "I sometimes think people might have such black holes too. We'll all disappear into our own black holes one day." The heartbreak and longing I felt surprised me.

On the days I ached with yearning for her, I kept repeating to myself, perhaps not in these exact words but in a similarly disjointed manner, that what I was missing wasn't Hayat Hanım per se—I only missed being with her. Our relationship used to fill up most of my time, and when it ended it left a void that I mistook for longing, in the same way that I always mistook for sorrow the puzzlement I felt in the face of changing circumstances—those, none of those were real feelings. All this ruminative thinking was based on a single notion—that Hayat Hanım wasn't the type of person one could long for; she wasn't someone whose absence one could grieve over. In an attempt to dull the pain inside, I settled for self-degradation. I did this over and over again.

Now that so much time has elapsed since, I allow myself to remember her without self-deception; her laugh, the unshakable optimism one only sees in the people who live to satisfy their instant desires, her nonchalance, her compassionate sense of irony, her ultimate disdain for both life and death, her glorious lovemaking, and the way she used to fling her ginger-gold hair—I remember and deeply yearn for all of this. I made peace with the fact that she was the most extraordinary and impressive person I had ever met. I saw the absurdity of being afraid of the feelings I had for her, and thus escaping from them, trying to reduce her in my mind. I have now come to know that one's ideas about what's right and what's wrong cannot overrule your feelings—emotions don't give a hoot about such judgments. I've experienced the great defeat and destruction at the end of personal battle. I've given up my weapons, surrendered to myself. And I know this: when I say *myself* I merely mean *my feelings*. But I didn't discover things about myself only—reading her letter over and over again I understood something, something that had never occurred to me before. She, too, tried to get away from me. I now know that her mysterious absences were part of an effort to escape. Perhaps she thought she had no right to affect the future of a man my age. She might not have realized that her efforts to spare me would end up harming me.

After Hayat Hanım disappeared, I called Sıla a couple of times, but she was busy too.

"Have you filled out the college admission forms for Canada?" she asked.

"Not yet," I said.

"OK, then."

On the third night, Hayat Hanım was there in her honey-colored dress. She was dancing in that familiar light, burning gold. I was drunk with joy.

During the intermission she came up to me and said, "Don't go anywhere. Let's grab a bite together." How she could be so calm, I had no idea. Her composure wounded me.

After the session, we went to eat among the sculptures. She was cheerful. We acted as if nothing had happened, but something had, and we both knew it.

I told her about Poet's magazine and my new job of co-pyediting articles, hoping that she would be intrigued and concerned and would change her mind about leaving me. That was a mistake. She got much more worried than I had presumed she might, and reacted in a way I had not expected.

"You're getting involved in risky affairs, Antony. It's best for you to get away as soon as possible. Go to Canada with that girl, she looks like a good person. Here you'll get into trouble. I wouldn't be able to live with myself if you ended up in prison."

I tried to calm her, "Nothing will happen to me," I said, "I'm not doing anything dangerous."

"Is that why that boy threw himself off the balcony?"

I didn't have an answer to that.

"It's time for you to leave this place, Antony. Trust me."

"Won't you miss me if I go away?"

I thought, only for a second, I saw a faint sneer on her lips.

"I'll miss you," she said.

She stroked my hand.

"Come on, eat your food, you're not eating."

We went to her apartment. She put on her short skirt and high-heeled slippers. Everything was the way it always used to be. We made love, we watched a documentary, we talked. Everything was the same as before, but I sensed a void, and that made me suspicious and sad. I didn't know what it was that was now lacking. Was it her face that froze momentarily in between smiles? Was it her getting out of bed sooner than usual? Was it her being less ironic? . . . There were subtle changes, but I felt they preceded a major shift. The image of a ship appeared in my mind—a large vessel getting ready with the tiniest of maneuvers for its final hawser to be withdrawn in order to leave the dock.

The weather was warmer now. Trees were in blossom. Playful clouds were passing over the city. The cool smell of the sea everywhere. But the joy of all of this could neither penetrate the walls of the buildings nor descend to the ground. The streets had a cold, dour look; no one smiled anymore. The street of the boardinghouse, which had been filled with guffawing people this time last year, was now mostly empty, with only a few folks around. Waiters waited hopelessly at the doors of restaurants.

The building was also in disarray. Tenants were fighting in the kitchen over who stole whose food from the fridge. Tea water no longer boiled in the samovar. Another tenant had stabbed Gülsüm with a knife. She was hospitalized. Bodyguard and I went to visit her; she cried when she saw us. The busboy with the thin mustache, who used to stay in one of the rooms on the ground floor, had moved into Poet's room.

I was still seeing both Hayat Hanım and Sıla, but not as frequently as I used to. They acted as if they were preparing both themselves and me for something I didn't want to put a name to. Sıla was corresponding with the university in Canada. She had sent all her documents and was waiting for a final approval from them. She didn't come to see the farmers. There was something dull about our conversations now; we didn't laugh as much as we used to. She had stopped asking me whether I had filled out the forms.

One day, I went to her college to meet her. We were walking side by side when a large car stopped next to us. Yakup opened the door and said, "Come on, get in." Sıla said, "Thank you, but the weather is nice, we're going to walk." Yakup didn't budge. He was so insistent that after a while we were embarrassed to say "No." We got into the car. Sıla sat in the back with Yakup, and in order not to crowd them, I sat in the front, next to the driver. Yakup was wearing a gray suit made of shimmery fabric. Around his neck was a loosened tie with yellow, purple, and lavender flowers on it, and a green handkerchief the size of a cabbage leaf hung from his coat pocket.

"How are you, Sılacığım," Yakup said without greeting me.

"Thank you, Yakup. I'm fine. How are you?"

"Just swell, Sılacığım. We got ourselves a highway job. Big job. Pretty big… How is Muammer Abi? Still working in the fruit market?"

"Yes," said Sıla, coldly.

"You told him to come to me if he needed anything, right? Did you give him my business card?"

"I did."

"If there's anything we can do to help…"

"I told him, Yakup."

There was silence.

"It's very nice outside," Yakup said. "Should we grab a bite at the seaside? A new restaurant just opened…"

Then he pointed at me. "That fellow can come too, if he'd like," he said. On hearing that line, *That fellow can come too*, Sıla and I looked at each other and instantly broke into laughter. The more we tried to control ourselves, the harder we laughed. What he said was simply too much for our nerves.

Yakup was furious.

"What's with the laughter?" he said. "Why are you chuckling? What's so funny?"

Sıla reached forward and tapped the driver on the shoulder. "Please stop here, Yakup," she said. The car stopped. As we got out, she said "Good day, Yakup." The car drove away, but we couldn't stop laughing.

"That was quite brutal," I said, still laughing.

"He deserved it," Sıla responded.

She looked at me and asked what the farmers were doing. "They miss you," I said.

"Let's go see if they're still on their way to a dance."

When we entered the room, "These guys are just like you," she said. "They're not going anywhere either."

As I opened the balcony door, I said, "I sent the form." I was lying, but at that moment I also decided to fill out the form and send it for real. Truth and untruth switched places so fast at times that it was hard for me to follow which was which.

"Really?"

"Really."

"This makes me so happy."

I realized how much I had missed her when we embraced. Sometimes our emotions escape us. We feel things, but we don't know how profound those feelings are. Then, all at once, we find ourselves at rock bottom and are surprised by how deeply we have fallen. The feelings we have for someone accumulate and intensify in their absence. Then, when we see them again, or touch them after a while, floodgates burst open, feelings drown us.

"Gather all your documents now, so that we can leave as soon as finals are over," she said while she smoked her cigarette. I hadn't seen her this happy for a long time. "There are squirrels in the campus," she said. "Hakan told me."

"I'll do it right away."

I said I would, but I didn't feel as certain as I was only a minute ago when I opened the balcony door. I tried to suppress the hesitation in my voice. Despite all my dithering I knew I would end up going with her. Everything was clearly flowing in one direction, and I didn't have the strength to resist it.

"How are we going to solve the money problem?" I asked.

"I've talked with Hakan. He'll lend us some at first. We'll pay him back later. Think about it, we'll be dealing with literature only, we'll be unfettered by all this nonsense."

Such an appealing reverie.

She held my hand firmly.

"These poor farmers will finally go somewhere. They are also exasperated with all this waiting."

"Wouldn't you like to wake up beside me in the morning?" she asked in a flirtatious tone I'd never heard her use before. I didn't know her voice was capable of such color: she generally seemed to disdain such gestures of femininity.

"Close the balcony door," she said. "It's chilly."

When she put out her cigarette, we made love again. Afterward, she whispered in my ear: "Don't be so sure that you know everything there is to know about me."

I dropped her off where she lived. I went straight back to the boardinghouse. Mümtaz was supposed to bring the articles I was going to proof that night, but no one brought anything. I went down to the kitchen to drink tea. The busboy with the thin mustache came in and looked at me.

"Waiting for someone?"

"Nope," I said. "Why do you ask?"

"You look like you're waiting for someone is all…"

"How's work going?" I asked.

"Just fine," he said.

"How is it *just fine*? The streets are desolate, no one is going to restaurants."

"The ones that do are more than enough for us."

There was no reason for it, but I wanted to hit him, break his bones, rub his face against the wall. *I'm going mad*, I thought, and left the kitchen in a hurry.

The next morning at Kaan Bey's class, I was unable to focus, but then he mentioned some names that piqued my interest.

"Let's assume D. H. Lawrence wasn't a writer and instead had been the only publisher on earth. Then the world would have never been able to read Tolstoy, because Lawrence didn't at all like Tolstoy. He found him immoral, in fact. Had Tolstoy been the only publisher on earth, then the world would not have been able to read Dostoevsky, because Tolstoy didn't like Dostoevsky… Had Dostoevsky been the only publisher, the world wouldn't have been able to read anyone, no writer whosoever, because Dostoevsky didn't like anyone else's work. Had Gide been the only publisher, we wouldn't have read Proust. Had Henry James been the only publisher, we wouldn't have read Flaubert…"

After the class, I went to the library, but I couldn't concentrate on any book. There was a session at the studio that night, and I was wondering if Hayat Hanım would come.

Before the program, I went by the boardinghouse. A little note on my door explained why the articles had not arrived. The magazine was closed. They would not be sending articles for me to proof anymore. I didn't know who wrote the note; there was no signature.

Hayat Hanım didn't come that night.

A woman in a turquoise minidress with a deep décolletage was singing. The figure of a leopard adorned the dress, a big cat charging from the woman's belly toward her breasts. In the audience, there were a larger number of somber-looking, low-spirited women than before. They obviously found it difficult to clap and dance to the tempo—they were clumsy but trying.

During the intermission, the blonde woman came near me.

"You're sitting all the way to the back, but the camera still keeps turning to you," she said. "I should sit by you. They might show me also."

"Sure, you're welcome to join me," I said. "Is that a good thing? To be on the screen?"

The off chance that someone I knew could pause at this show while channel surfing and spot me in the audience worried me all the time. I couldn't fathom her desire to be seen.

"Why wouldn't it be a good thing? You're seen on TV."

"What happens when they see you on TV?"

The woman stared at my face as if she were saying *You are a prize idiot!*

"You're seen on TV," she repeated.

She looked utterly confident that she had explained herself well. She wanted to be seen. She wanted to stick her head out from among a dreary crowd of eight billion people, even if it was for a moment only. Then she leaned in as if she was telling me a secret. "Rumor has it that they'll end this show," she said. "Have you heard anything?"

"I haven't," I said.

"Hayat Hanım is again a no-show today," she said then. "What's up with her?"

"I don't know," I said.

"Don't you two see each other outside as well?"

I didn't answer. The woman wasn't at all offended by my silence.

"She would know what's going on," she said.

Again, I kept quiet, and she didn't miss the chance to make me pay for my silence.

"Remzi must have told her."

I looked down so that she wouldn't see my expression. After the intermission, she came and sat near me. Sure enough, both our faces were soon on the screen. She nudged me with joy: "Look! I told you."

When the session was over, I walked alone through the streets. No one was out and about. As I approached the boardinghouse I saw the men with bats. They were in a good mood, poking one another with their bats. I turned into an alley and took the long way home to escape their prying eyes. Lately, any sighting of them filled me with an uncontrollable rage. Walking away on empty streets eventually calmed me. I forgot where I was heading. I was lost in my thoughts. When I finally raised my head and looked up, I found myself on the street of old booksellers. But the arcade was gone. Disappeared from the earth. There was a mud-filled ditch in its place.

I had come to this arcade many times over the years, browsing the shops and inhaling dust and the smell of old paper, bought many of my favorite books here, observing on their pages the traces left by their owners before me, imagining what might have gone through their minds when they read those paragraphs, leaving my own traces.

They had demolished the building. The old bookseller had told me they would, but I must not have believed the place could disappear altogether. I felt violated, somehow. *I need to get away from here*, I thought. They had entered my home at night, destroyed everything, written threats on the ruined walls that they would be back. That's how it felt to me.

I sat on the curb. I was like a commander sitting on a rock, defeated, his army gone, waiting for the enemy troops to find and kill him. I was learning what defeat was, what it was to be overpowered, what desolation, dashed hopes, and desperation meant. Sıla was right. We had to escape to survive, we had to get out of this place and go away.

I don't know how long I sat there, but I was unsteady when I got up. I went back to the boardinghouse. All the lights were out—even the kitchen, where the lamp was always left on, was dark; the samovar was cold. I went up to my room. I turned on the light. I opened the balcony door. The night sky was clear, starry; the air smelled like spring.

My farmers, unaware of what had been unfolding outside, were on their way to a dance. I grabbed the dictionary of mythology to check what my gods and goddesses were up to. They were driving mad the ones they fell in love with in order to ensure their loyalty. Cybele drove Attis mad, because she was jealous. Artemis drove Aura mad to take revenge. Dionysus drove scores of women mad. Packed in just two back-to-back pages of the dictionary was so much madness, so much tragedy. I would drive Hayat Hanım mad to make her forget the day she saw me with Sıla. To make her overcome her frustration, her chagrin, which she believed she had to hide from me just because she was older. To stop her from worrying about me. I would do that if I could. If I knew there would be a chance to erase that sentence—*I saw you with that girl*—I wouldn't stop at anything. I passed out with my clothes on and the balcony door open. I woke up aching all over.

I went to school. Students had gathered on the campus lawn. I heard a roaring sound and immediately knew something bad had happened. I grabbed someone by the arm; "What's going on here?"

"They arrested Nermin Hanım and Kaan Bey this morning."

"Why?"

"They had signed a petition. All fifty of the professors who signed it were taken from their homes before dawn."

I didn't join the crowd. I went to the student administration and got the documents I needed for Canada. I put them in a large envelope I bought at the campus store. I called Sıla. I wanted to mail them with her. We went to the post office together.

"Why don't we scan these pages and send them in an email instead?" she asked.

"I like it better this way," I said.

She curled her lips. "You're odd." We mailed the envelope.

"They've arrested Nermin Hanım and Kaan Bey."

"I know," she said. "They arrested five of our professors too. We're leaving at the right time. We can't live here, we really can't."

"I'm very upset," I said. "They'll treat them badly there. Especially Nermin Hanım…"

I told her the old booksellers' arcade had been demolished. "Last night, I understood what it is like to be crushed," I said. "I had never felt defeat so intensely before."

"We'll forget all of this once we're gone," she said.

"It's not so easy to forget."

She saw how absolutely sad I was. She took my arm. "Let's go to our place," she said. She had never called my room "our place" before.

"Consolation sex?" I snickered.

"Is there a better way of consoling a sad person? If you know a better way, tell me and I'll do that."

Her fingers pressing against my arm reassured me that she sensed the love and companionship I felt for her. Ours was the kind of intimacy one would happily get used to. Had images of Hayat Hanım not been occupying my mind, I could have felt happy even!

"Which perfume do you like?"

"Why do you ask?"

"I'll buy it for you as soon as we land in Canada."

That evening after I dropped Sıla off I went to the studio. Once again, Hayat Hanım wasn't there.

12

When she didn't show up for ten days in a row I did something I had never done before and tried to call her on the phone, but her line was disconnected. A mechanical voice, prickling my lungs, announced that her number was no longer valid, and with that everything became metallic, meaningless. I couldn't stand it any longer. Taking my chance at being rebuked, demeaned, or taunted, risking being damaged even by what I might encounter, I went to her apartment.

When she opened the door she had a long, loose housedress on, flat slippers. Her hair was held up with a pin, and she wasn't wearing any makeup. I had never seen her without makeup. I don't know how and when she managed to do it, but she always had a touch of foundation on her face. "Reality is the enemy of women, Antony," she used to say, "you know, makeup is allowed even during wartime." Her face had become translucent, its fine lines deeper, looking surprisingly innocent. Her eyes were tired, their teasing twinkle gone.

I realized that she had crawled into her solitary place during the days I hadn't seen her. However, this time she couldn't come out of that isolation with her usual ease, as if something was holding her up. There was a foreignness to her expression. It felt like I was disturbing her. I was embarrassed.

"I was worried about you," I said.

Slowly adapting herself, she spoke in a calm voice. "Come. Sit down."

The apartment had been aired recently; it was bright, but the vases were empty. She must not have left the place for quite a while. "I was worried," I said again. I didn't know what to say exactly.

"OK, Antony," she said, now smiling, "have a seat."

"Are you all right?" I asked.

"I've got a bit of a cold."

"And your phone was off."

"I didn't have the energy to talk…"

She wasn't angry that I had come to see her. She had greeted me as if I had done the most natural thing.

"Let me make you some coffee," she said.

"Should I help?"

"No. You sit down."

I sat down. She brought the coffee and asked: "How are you doing? I was worried about you too. Are you good?"

"I'm good," I said, sounding anxious, restless.

"Come on, make yourself comfortable," she said. "Why are you perching on the edge of your seat like that? You will fall off."

I leaned back. I was looking at her, trying to read her feelings. Was she chagrined, was she upset with me, was she resentful, had she given up on me…I could see no clues on her face about how she felt, I only saw the fatigue in her eyes. She was looking at me. She looked like she was also trying to see something. We were searching for signs in each other's faces. Like a man on the open sea looking at the horizon, I was trying to discern whether a moving shadow in the distance was a small wave or a big fish, whether the woeful shadow I thought I had seen in the corners of her eyes and lips was real or not. I realized that I had wanted to see a certain sorrow on that face. Now I also wanted joy at seeing me to complement that sorrow.

"Why are you looking at me like that?"

"Like what?"

"As if you're seeing me for the first time...Are you surprised I'm old?"

"You are not old," I said. "On the contrary. You look very young."

"You're such a liar, Antony," she said with a chuckle. "But you're as kind as ever...You have a genuine kindness of heart, you should never lose that."

"I'm not lying," I said. "You are Queen Cleopatra, forever young."

She smiled, and for the first time I saw an unmistakable sorrow in her smile.

"Rather than a queen in Egypt, I should have been a mare in Poland," she said. "Sometimes it's better to be a horse than a royal."

Then, as if she was angry with herself for saying those things, she waved her hand in the air. "Whatever," she said. "What have you been doing? When will you go?"

"Nothing decided," I said. "I couldn't sort out the money problem. I'm not as certain that I'll be going."

"You should go. This place isn't safe anymore. They must have you on their list. I couldn't bear it if something happens to you. Not that…"

"You're exaggerating."

"Ah, Antony. Who would have thought we'd end up with *you* as the crazy one and *me* the sensible?"

She crossed her legs, her skin showing for an instant under her skirt. That much was enough to arouse me. Like a sapling planted and grown in her soil, maturing in her climate, with her water and her wind, I was dependent on her. Spotting her from a distance in a crowded airport, a train station, or an outdoor rally would be enough to arouse me. She was my wizard Merlin, she was my goddess Hecate. I couldn't break free of her spell: no one else could give me the kind of happiness she did. I knew that in my heart. Being so dependent on her also gave me an odd sense of reassurance; it made me believe I would never lose her.

She knew me well. She knew what my eyes were saying.

"What's up, Antony?"

My uneasiness was gone. I had gotten my confidence back. "What do you think?"

"Not now," she laughed. "I'm exhausted… We'll make up for it when I get better."

She was turning me down for the first time. "Don't sulk," she said, "I'm telling you we'll do it another time."

Then she was serious again. "Why are you still here? Is it the money?"

"There's that too, but..."

"What did Sıla do?" she asked as if it was an unimportant question.

"She completed her preparations. She's going."

"Smart girl."

We stopped talking. The silence lingered. With her vases empty, the apartment looked empty too. It was like we were in a train station, where whatever would be said had to be said quickly, but there were too many things to say and not all of them could fit in such a narrow interval of time. Unsaid, these words stuck in my windpipe, tightening my throat.

"Have you watched any new documentaries?" I managed to say.

"I have been tired lately. I couldn't watch a thing."

"Who takes care of you when you're sick?"

"I take care of myself."

"Should I take care of you? I can stay here and help you heal. You tell me what to do, I'll do it. I can cook for you."

"Ah, Antony," she whimpered... Then she added: "I prefer to be alone when I'm sick. I don't want you to see me sick, because if you do, you might leave me for good."

"In sickness and in health," I chuckled.

"Sometimes only in health," she said softly.

I wanted to insist, but I knew that would be in vain. It was as if something stood between us, something with a mind of its own, bigger than us. No matter what we did, we couldn't overcome that. An intangible, invisible wall had been built.

Flexing, strong. When we touched that wall, it pushed each of us back in opposite directions.

"You should go now," she said. "I'm going to take a nap."

"You don't want me here?"

"I'll get better in a few days," she said. "I'm really exhausted now."

I got up. She had already walked toward the door...I stopped and looked at her. I reached and took off her hairpin. Her ginger-gold hair fell over her shoulders. She looked at me without moving.

I stepped out and she closed the door gently behind me.

Going down the stairs, I thought about the expression on her face just before she closed the door. What was that? It looked like the gaze of an oracle who saw the future, duly accepting what lay ahead, forgoing any acts of rebellion, any kind of resistance. I also detected in her face the subtle, vaguely woeful smile of someone who has submitted herself to fate.

I felt like my insides were being ripped out. I tried to find comfort in her words, *I'll get better in a few days.* She never felt the need to explain things or make excuses, so she never lied. She would be back in a few days.

Three days later I found a bank notice stuck on my door. Someone had wired me money. The sender's name was illegible. The note on it said, "For the Canada trip." I went to the bank. I gave them the notice. They took me back to see a personal banker. A well-groomed young woman. She took the notice and looked it up on her computer.

"They wired a hundred thousand liras to your name," she said.

I was shaken, exultant. The kind of pure joy that a shipwrecked person would feel at the moment he reached the land. "I'm saved," I thought. I forgot about everything and everyone for a moment—there was only me, and I was saved. My poverty was over, and with it everything that had happened since my dad had died. Everyone I met, everything I felt was deleted, erased without a trace.

With a selfish presence of mind, I bought U.S. dollars with the money, opened an account, and put the sum in there. I left the bank with a great sense of relief and peace.

It took me more than a few days to grasp what had in fact happened, what was happening to me. Suddenly, it exploded in my mind: *She sold her car. She's gone*, I thought, *she left me. I'll never see her again*. I couldn't swallow, I couldn't breathe, I was dizzy. Afraid that I might stumble and fall, I sat on the curb. The street had become an ash-colored vortex, swirling and pulling me in.

When I got myself somewhat together, I called her from the first pay phone I found. That mechanical voice I had come to hate answered: "This number is no longer valid."

I hailed a cab and went to her place. Her car wasn't there. Another car had taken its parking space. The curtains were drawn.

I rang the bell. I rang the bell. I rang the bell.

The door didn't open.

13

During the first days of her absence, I was like a blind man. I lived in a constant twilight; the city was erased from my memory, I didn't remember the street names, I couldn't find my way. I was either sleeping or going for walks: I couldn't stand being still when I was awake, I had difficulty breathing and had to sigh repeatedly as I walked. Whenever I thought I would never see Hayat Hanım again, I felt myself confined to a cell with no doors or windows, my mind fluttering to get out of that terrifying place. The things I could have said to her but didn't constantly squeezed my insides.

I wasn't thinking of her teasing gaze, prankish but benign jokes, not even her magnificent nakedness; I only remembered her words that left a sad trace in me, *Pick a moment... Sometimes being a mare is better than being a queen*; her weeping in bed for a little dead child. My unhappiness formed a thick shell, not allowing even the tiniest image of joy to seep in. And thinking of the times she was sad made my heartbreak even worse. Instead of trying to pull out the knife I was stabbed with, I was for whatever reason trying to push it in deeper.

I watched myself in bewilderment, somewhat with disdain. *Yes*, Hayat Hanım was very important to me, I was addicted to her body, her nakedness, her ease. I longed for her, desired her, and was jealous of her, but secretly, I had also scorned her ignorance about literature, her intimate ties with lower-class men, her fibs about her father, her suggestive dancing in public, and her ease at being an extra in a show watched in the slums. My contempt had given me a sneaking sense of safety, and therefore I had selfishly kept it alive. The feelings I had for her used to seem like part of a game to me. Even though I missed her during her mysterious absences, I had brought myself to believe that my sense of longing wasn't all that genuine, and so I shouldn't be scared by it. I had also believed my attachment to her was physical, and while I always knew I would feel a sense of deprivation if I lost her, I was secretly confident she would be easy to overcome. But now that I had lost her it was my soul rather than my flesh that felt the wound. My consciousness, my whole being almost, was hurting. I didn't understand how that could happen. When did Hayat Hanım take hold of my entire consciousness, my entire memory, and settle herself there? How could it be that losing her felt akin to losing everything? On which day, and at which hour, had this woman—whom I couldn't introduce to either my mother or my friends, whom I was always secretly ashamed to be seen with—taken hold of me so profoundly, conquering my whole being, that I now felt like I would die without her? I didn't know the answer to any of these questions. Something that wasn't supposed to happen was happening, an experience that wasn't supposed to be experienced. I couldn't understand myself, my feelings or thoughts. When had that relationship ceased to be just a game and become real? Sometimes I thought for hours, going over all the things we had done together and tried to find *that single moment*. I couldn't find it. I was angry with her. She had taken me into her life with such ease, and now she had discarded me in the same manner. This had always been a game for her. She had trapped me. She had made everything seem like a game. She laughed at everything, she laughed wickedly, teasingly, so beautifully. Because she didn't mind anything, I had thought I wouldn't mind anything either. *At the very most we die*, she used to say, but she never told me we would suffer when that *very most* happened and we were dying. She scorned pain, and I thought I could scorn it too. *Pick a moment*, she had said. She didn't scorn that moment, yet I didn't notice that, I didn't imagine a single moment could become my life. She took me to a place beyond humanity, history, and literature, the land of deities, and I thought I'd always stay there. She had deceived me like God deceived Adam and banished me from her Eden for my original sin. When I asked her *Who are you?* she said the same thing God said to Moses: *I am who I am*. Moses didn't know a thing about God, and I didn't know a thing about her. I missed her. She didn't care for me. I couldn't live without her. How did that happen? *There are no rules to this*, she had told me once. There are no rules to this. She hadn't read even a single novel. Were there really no rules, none at all?

I missed hearing a human voice at times, I missed talking to people, but I couldn't stand speaking to anyone for long, and soon wanted to retreat inside myself. Sıla was busy getting ready for the trip. I knew I had no other choice than leaving this place. I felt I couldn't live here without the possibility of seeing Hayat Hanım. This city intensified my loneliness.

I called my mother on the phone. "What's the matter?" she asked the second she heard my voice.

"I'm OK," I said.

"You don't sound OK."

"I'm fine, Mom."

A brief silence.

"I'm going to Canada," I said. "But I'm getting on the bus tonight to come visit you, I'll tell you all about it when I'm there."

I bought a ticket for the midnight bus. I went back to the boardinghouse to rest a little bit. I saw Emir and Tevhide in the kitchen. Tevhide came to me running, and she held my hand: "We're moving out."

"I'll miss you," I said.

She giggled. "Really?"

"Really."

"In that case, I'll miss you too."

I looked at Emir; the vein under his eye was twitching. I didn't ask where they were moving to, and he didn't volunteer that information. We shook hands. I wished him good luck.

"To you too," he said. "Perhaps we'll see each other again someday."

"Perhaps."

I went up to my room. Their plan to move had upset me more than I thought it would. Everyone was leaving. I lay down but couldn't sleep. I got up and stepped out to the balcony. The street was deserted.

The bus departed right on time. We drove through the city, then the lights became dimmer. I leaned my head against the window. I must have passed out. Then I woke up abruptly, thinking *I will never see Hayat Hanım again.* The lack of possibility terrified me, a helplessness resembling death in life. I knew there was always some hope as long as we lived, but one needed inner strength to be able to keep that hope alive, a strength I didn't have. I was consumed.

I got off the bus at eight in the morning. Half an hour later I was at my mother's house.

She had taken pains to prepare a huge breakfast. I started to eat with appetite as if seeing my mom had persuaded my body to continue to live. I told her about Canada, about my plans and Sıla. "I'm thinking of living there," I said. "Once I settle, you can come too, maybe. We can both live there."

"We'll see about that, Son," she said.

She looked better than the last time I saw her, but she still seemed to carry a sadness inside. She might never laugh again, I thought. It was as if a vital organ had been removed from her body, taking away her ability to laugh, that's what I saw in her big, dark eyes. The woman I remembered to be always full of joy was now reduced to a polite, melancholic smile.

After breakfast, we went out and sat in a café by the sea. I was peaceful, calm. We talked about my father. There was a loving sorrow in her voice, she liked talking about him. We spent two very good hours together. Then, all of a sudden, for no apparent reason, I felt as if an iron door was shut inside me, its lock turned. I had difficulty breathing and wanted to go back at once.

My mother didn't insist that I stay, but she came all the way to the terminal to see me off. When I was getting on the bus, she said, "You should go away, Son! Perhaps, later, I'll come too." I fell asleep as soon as the bus moved, and didn't wake up during the trip. It was past midnight when I arrived at the boarding-house. I sat on the balcony, having a hard time breathing.

After a while, I felt very thirsty. I went down to the kitchen to get a drink of water. The new tenant, an elderly man, was sitting all by himself at the long table. He had a gray suit and a black necktie on. His hair was white as snow. He had recently moved in. He never said a word to anyone. Sometimes he came to the kitchen dragging his feet, took a cup of tea, and left. Everyone thought he was mad, although he didn't say or do anything to suggest that. Madness was etched on his face. His facial lines were in disarray somehow, flowing and dripping like splashes of watercolor on paper, unable to hold on to any expression. There was no trace of emotion or thought on that face. His eyes were always wet, as if he had been weeping.

We stared at each other in the empty kitchen. I saw the madness in his face. I don't know what he saw in mine. But whatever it was that he saw, the lines on his face suddenly became defined, and now he could barely hide an expression, something that resembled pity.

"Come, sit down," he said.

His voice was soft but authoritative.

I sat across from him. For a while, neither of us spoke. Then he began to tell his story:

"I used to have a stamp shop. I used to deal in rare stamps. Three months ago, a rumor was spread around that a misprinted stamp had become available in the market. There's nothing more precious in the world than a stamp with a unique error. Every stamp dealer's dream is to find a stamp like that, one that is the sole remaining example of its kind. One day a fellow philatelist whom I trusted very much came to my shop and said he had found the rumored stamp. 'I can't afford it,' he said. 'If you have money, you buy it.' I had hit the jackpot. I sold everything, my house, my car, my shop, everything. I purchased the misprinted stamp my friend brought. Then, I began to wait. One day a very wealthy collector came to see the stamp. He examined it for a long time, then said, 'This is a fake.' And I said, 'No way, that's not possible, I invested my entire life in this stamp.' He suggested I consult an expert. I agreed. The next day he came back with the expert. It was the friend who sold me the stamp. He examined it and said it was a forgery. I must have been so blinded with ambition that I had not been able to tell it was a fake."

He took out a small envelope from his pocket, held it upside down, and a small stamp fell on the table.

"The world's most precious stamp," he said.

Then he added in a calm voice: "But it is fake... One should find a genuine example of this. If you ever find it, never lose it."

"What did you do to the friend who sold you the stamp?"

His facial lines got blurry again, began to drip. The expression was gone. His eyes turned blank as if he couldn't see me anymore.

He put the stamp back in the envelope. "So, that is *that*..." he said before he got up and left, dragging his feet. I had no idea why he told me this specific story, but I was moved. What affected me wasn't so much the man's ordeal, though. I was touched by his using the last ounce of his strength to retreat from the edge of madness, if only for a moment, in order to be able to engage me in a conversation, which he must have reckoned might console me. He used all his will-power to tell me the only story he was able to keep in his mind. Realizing how desperate I must look to gain even a madman's mercy could have been upsetting, but I didn't feel that way. A man with one foot in the grave had used whatever remained in his hands to show me sympathy and this did me good. I calmed down. I went to my room and straight to bed, without turning the light on. I was afraid to see my reflection in the mirror. Looking at the face that, even for a moment only, had given pause to a man on his path to madness might also make me change course and join him on that track. Those days agonizing over such a possibility didn't feel unnatural to me.

Two days later, Sıla and I went to buy our tickets. She was talking about the future with a thrill in her voice. I liked listening to her—I was trying to make myself believe that in Canada I would forget everything and become a new man. I had to believe in something, I had to hold on to a dream; that was the only way to stop my sense of dying. We were going to leave in two weeks.

One night when I came back from a long walk on streets whose names I couldn't remember, I turned on the light in my room and saw an envelope had been slipped under the door. I opened it, began to read the letter inside:

Why haven't you left yet? Yes, I'm watching you. I come by now and then to see if you're gone. I'm leaving tomorrow. I'll be going deep into the country. I won't come back any time soon. Perhaps never...

Yes, I've been sad. Very sad. You wanted me to be sad. And so I was. I had forgotten what being sad was like. I was reminded of it. Being sad is forgetting that the earth is a mere piece of rock that tilts every twenty thousand years.

People also forget this fact when they're happy. Happiness and sadness are strangely similar—both depend on forgetting the facts. Thanks to you, I experienced both of these states of mind.

Get away from this place. Take Sıla with you and go away. It will do me good to know that you're safe and well. I worry about you. You also reminded me what it was to be afraid.

Whatever you do, whomever you love, a "moment" from me will remain with you, right? Don't forget to pick that moment and keep it safe somewhere inside you. I still want this.

My handsome, my kind Antony…

Like Poet, Hayat Hanım, too, had slipped through my fingers; I couldn't hold on to her. She had slid into the void, she wasn't coming back, and never again would I be the same.

Now that I would never see her again, I was learning she did love me. The sense of joy and victory I felt in reading this confession hidden in her lines, a happiness so peculiar in those circumstances, ended up exacerbating my pain, my defeat, and my unhappiness.

Had I spoken the words I had withheld from her, my entire future would have been different. The things I left unsaid, or only half said, hit against the wall of life and changed their direction.

Had I said those words, everything would have been different.

But I hadn't been able to.

14

Summer is over, replaced by the translucent cool of autumn mornings. It has been three months since Sıla left. I couldn't go. I changed my mind at the last minute. I decided to search for my misplaced happiness here, for where I had lost it was the only place I could find it again. Packing all my past experiences in a suitcase and tossing it backward in time would also rob me of my future, I thought. Had I done that, something would always be missing in my life, and I would have been forever disabled by that sense of absence. I knew I couldn't go on living like that, forever dismembered, forever trying to find the severed piece, always incomplete.

Time passes. Life is teaching me what's left behind as time passes. What's left behind is what I carry in me, my personal history. Things I could have never imagined a year ago are now part of that history. Going through so many things in such a short time comes with a cost, and I'm paying it.

It was difficult for me to tell Sıla I wasn't going to go with her. I avoided the conversation for days. I ran the back-and-forth in my mind maybe a thousand times—I said this, she said that. Still, I could never have anticipated that our actual conversation would be as devastating and painful as it was.

I said to her all at once I wasn't going to Canada, I was going to return my ticket. She didn't grasp what I was saying at first, I think. Then she lowered her eyes. I watched her right hand squeeze her left, her knuckles turning white with pressure.

"Is it because of that woman?" she asked.

I remember feeling unsteady, as if I would fall. I had to hold on to the table. I also remember musing to myself that inside every woman lived an oracle. While I failed to grasp what I actually saw, women grasped what they had never seen. They decoded the secrets, yet they took their time to let me know about it.

"Which woman?" I asked.

"You know... That old woman."

Then she said something I never expected to hear: "Did you think she couldn't live without you?"

The question betrayed a wounded heart, something I thought I would never see in her. I used to believe that physical beauty always protected certain women, that it safeguarded them against being harmed emotionally. Yet Sıla was hurt. I never thought I had the power to hurt a woman that beautiful, and it gave me an odd feeling, hard to describe, like guilt about having taken something that didn't belong to me, or having masqueraded as someone else.

For a brief moment, I felt the urge to come clean and tell her everything, but *honesty isn't always just. One should decide carefully when to be honest.* The truth might have hurt her even more, so I chose to tell her a lie she could feel safe with.

"It has nothing to do with her, I don't even see her..."

What I said was partially true, at least.

She looked at my face. Such a rare beauty she had—I might never see anything like it again. Had she and I met before, when my father was still alive, when she and I were both rich, everything could have turned out differently, I suppose. She was the kind of woman I dreamed of as a child. We would have got married, perhaps. And if one of us were to eventually leave the other, it wouldn't have been me. However, for reasons that are mostly beyond my grasp, that wasn't how things turned out. People don't always understand themselves. Or their actions.

"OK, then," she said as she grabbed her purse and got up. She took a few steps, then she turned back to me, and delivering the final blow as gracefully as one would expect from her, said: "Don't be sad."

With that, she hurried away. Her brisk walk reminded me of the time she stood against the wind with her arms stretched out. Suddenly, I felt such a profound affection and sense of longing for her that, for a moment, I thought I would change my mind and run after her. She got into a cab before I could move. I watched the car drive away. It was a beautiful day, the sky bright blue, with tiny clouds drifting along and seagulls flying in circles, picking on each other. The strong aroma of silverberry flowers had taken over the street. Everything I saw, everything I heard and smelled, all the life going on around me in all of its glory, made the melancholy of separation worse for me and increased my loneliness.

Sıla's departure was like an aftershock following a major earthquake—it knocked down whatever was still standing, and I was buried in a massive pile of debris. As always, I took shelter in my classes, in literature. After receiving Hayat Hanım's letter, I hadn't been able to bring myself to go to the studio anymore, and some time later, they shut down the TV channel. I got a job at my university's library. I spend most of my time on campus these days. At lunchtime, I take my sandwich and sit and eat with my classmates under the trees. Usually I am the talker in the group, and I help others with their assignments. That makes me feel good about myself.

I look at my reflection in the mornings. Those terrible signs of melancholy, which could divert people from their journey into madness, aren't there anymore. My face has a peaceful and mellow expression now, a bit unusual for my age, perhaps. I look like an old man. Women find the contrast between my looks and my age oddly appealing. They want to lift the skin off my face as they would open a book's cover, and look inside. I smile at them. "There's nothing interesting about my life," I say.

Nermin Hanım and Kaan Bey are still in prison. No one knows when they will be released. We talk about them often. After everything that has happened to me, I think I have finally come up with an answer to Kaan Bey's question about clichés and coincidences: Being born is a cliché, dying is a cliché. Love is a cliché, separation is a cliché, longing is a cliché, betrayal is a cliché, denying your feelings is a cliché, vulner-ability is a cliché, fear is a cliché, poverty is a cliché, the passage of time is a cliché, injustice is a cliché ... And these clichés harbor the truth, the kind that can devastate a man. People live, suffer, and die with clichés.

When you'll be born, when you'll die, whom you'll fall in love with, whom you'll part ways with, when you'll be scared, whether you'll be poor or not, are all coincidental. When someone close to us gets sick, dies, and leaves us behind, when that terrifying *coincidence* finds us, the cliché no longer matters. Coincidences determine our destiny, which for its part prevents us from grasping that everything that happens to us is but a series of clichés. Because it makes no sense to rebel against clichés, we rebel against coincidences: *why me*, we ask, *why her, why now.*

We shouldn't try to get away from ordinary truths—which are nothing but a series of clichés and coincidences anyway. Instead, we need to submerge ourselves in them, making our way down, deeper and deeper. For those depths are where literature cohabits with life.

Mümtaz and his friends are publishing a new magazine. I edit their articles and write some of my own, without a byline. I've increasingly taken to writing. I feel like I have discovered a staircase, its top steps reaching the sky, its base firmly placed underground. Writing makes me feel I have the power and unrestricted freedom to flex and reshape both time and space. Now, for the first ever, I've found a universe in which I can determine the entire state of affairs. Writing doesn't open the door only to great internal freedom, however. It also opens the door to outside dangers, I'm aware of that. Every day at dawn I wake up in a sweat and look out my window to see whether there are police cars outside. Fear vibrates in me like a stretched wire. This, I believe, is part of my eternal debt to Poet for not having been able to save him.

I'm used to being lonely now and to longing. No complaints there. I've learned to swallow the poison in the honey quietly. Hayat Hanım taught me this, as well as so many other things.

Two lines from the Shakespeare sonnet we read in class resonate in my mind all the time:

Thus have I had thee as a dream doth flatter:
In sleep a king but waking no such matter.

I miss her. In my mind, I see her, deep asleep. When I woke up the first night we had spent together, I couldn't remember where I was at first. The lamp in the living room was on. Its light traveled through the long corridor, losing some of its brightness at each doorframe, wall beam, floor tile, and small rug on its route, and arrived at the dark bedroom as its reduced self, in little droplets: a droplet of light surfed on Hayat Hanım's ginger-gold mane, which left her face partially uncovered and fell over her shoulders. She had put her right arm on the pillow and leaned her head against her right hand, stretching her left arm forward, the roundness of her shoulder peeking out. The comforter creased and curved on her body. I lifted it gently and looked underneath at her nakedness, the droplets of light pooling around her slightly thick waist, her firm back, her wide hips, her strong legs, one of which she had pulled up. In the dim light of the room her body shimmered on its own. As luminescent as ivory, I thought, like moonlight, like silver, like the silvery body of poplars under the summer sun, like the reddish coral of the South Seas. I had just made love to her. Making love to her wasn't the simple, ordinary thing I used to think it was. It was a magic cloak woven in delicate Chinese silk, embroidered with images of concubines, dragons, warriors, phoenixes, flames, flowers, clouds, cliffs, and mountain peaks. When you wore that cloak you could see what went on beyond the sky. The part of her face I could see between her arm and hair was peaceful; there was a calm innocence to it, not a hint of that sardonic, nonchalant look she had when she talked, nor the passionate expression that emerged when she made love. It was a face that called for compassion, a face one would be inspired to protect. And I was so inspired. She had such a wide range of moods, she touched life at so many different places, that it was impossible for me to understand which was the *real* her. All of her images, each one strikingly different, keep floating about in my mind now, without touching one another. Hard to fathom that a single person could take up so much mental space.

Every evening without fail, no matter what happens, I go to her street and look at her windows. The curtains are fading slowly. But new curtains haven't replaced them. No one else has moved into her apartment.

This gives me hope.

I dream about seeing that amber light there again one day. I will see those curtains illuminated.

I am waiting.

I am here.

About the Author and Translator

AHMET ALTAN, born in 1950, is one of Turkey's most important writers. In the purge following the failed coup of July 2016, Altan was sent to prison pending trial for giving "subliminal messages" in support of overthrowing the government. In February 2018 he was sentenced to life in prison without parole. Fifty-one Nobel laureates signed an open letter to President Erdoğan calling for Altan's release. His memoir *I Will Never See the World Again* was published by Other Press in 2019. Altan was released from prison in April 2021.

YASEMIN ÇONGAR is the cofounder and director of P24, a not-for-profit platform for independent journalism in Istanbul. She is also the founder of *K24*, a Turkish literary review, and of the Istanbul Literature House. An editor, essayist, and translator, Çongar is the author of four books in Turkish.